Beyond Ever After

ONCE UPON A BABY, BOOK THREE

Elle Wright

D0707177

Beyond Ever After
Copyright @ 2020 by Elle Wright
Paperback ISBN: 978-0-9994213-5-2

Excerpt from *Irresistible Temptation*
copyright @ 2020 by Elle Wright
Excerpt from *Her Little Secret*
copyright @ 2020 by Elle Wright

Elle Wrights Books, LLC
Ypsilanti, Michigan
www.ElleWright.com
Editor:
Nicole Falls
Cover Design:
Sherelle Green

❀ Created with Vellum

Ryleigh Sullivan has no plans on following through with the next Best Friends Challenge, especially when that challenge includes babies, bottles and back rubs. Well, she'd take the back rubs, but she may be down a husband if Martin doesn't get it through his sexy head that she's not ready to be a mother. The more he talks about it, the more she realizes they may never see eye to eye on parenthood. It's never fun when sex becomes a game of what if. Especially when their marriage has been the best kind of love so far.

For my girls, my lit sisters! Love y'all!

Acknowledgments

Woooo!!! I'm so grateful!

First, I want to thank God for being everything I need.

To my husband and children, thanks for understanding, for encouraging me to write even when I'm tired. I love you so much.

To my sista friends, Angela, Sherelle, and Sheryl; I'm so glad we tackled this Best Friends Challenge!! Love you!

A special shout-out to the amazing readers , bloggers, and awesome writers that I've met on this journey. There would be no "Elle Wright" without your love and encouragement, your enthusiasm and understanding.

Dear Reader

Wow! I cannot tell you how much I LOVED revisiting these characters. I loved them so much! I especially enjoyed collaborating with my lit sisters!

What started out as a quick, fun read quickly transformed into something a little more serious, but heartfelt. Ryleigh and Martin took me through some thangs with this one. But I enjoyed the ride. I hope you do, too.

For the best reading experience, make sure you read all of the #Baby books in order. Trust me, you won't regret it.

Love,
    Elle
    www.ellewright.com

The Pact

Where the hell is my bra?

Ryleigh scanned the floor. The last several minutes spent riding Martin's dick were hot and all, but she hated to be late. The christening started in less than an hour and she had no dress, no bra, and messy-as-fuck hair. Her bestie would maim her if she failed to make it on time.

Two children later, Ava Prescott-Sullivan was still as bossy and demanding as she'd been on her wedding day. Tight dresses, wedding favors, uncomfortable shoes, stupid ass ex-boyfriends... *Yeah, I still think weddings suck.* There were a couple of good things to come out of that warm September day almost four years ago—time with her best friends, seeing one of the most important people in her life get her happily ever after, and the man standing behind her. Martin Sullivan, aka fine as hell, aka sexy-ass muthafucka, aka her permanent plus one, aka her husband.

Ryleigh was a realist. The thought of finding her one true love at a wedding was cliché, definitely corny, and never going to happen. Until it did. After countless pictures, after standing in front of the entire Rosewood

Heights, South Carolina community in high heels—she'd thrown those things away as soon as the coast was clear—she'd watched her bestie marry Owen Sullivan. Throw in a few margaritas, a couple shots of tequila, a crazy ass Best Friends Challenge, running into a never forgotten one-night-stand who just happened to be Owen's first cousin, and the rest was history.

Now she was happily married to the man who'd just made her scream his name over and over again. Her impressive hubby—in life and with his dick—made every hard time, every bad outcome, every disappointment she'd ever felt better. He was the best thing to ever happen to her. For that, she owed her best friends the world. Well… that tequila and that tight, albeit sexy dress had played a critical role, too.

"Shit, what did you do with my bra?" She tossed a glance at Martin. He buttoned his slacks and grinned at her. "Eat it?"

She picked up her discarded dress off the floor—the one she was supposed to be wearing to the ceremony and the one Martin had literally ripped off her body before they could even make it out of their hotel suite. Who knew black lace would turn her husband into a sex-crazed lunatic? *I did.* Ryleigh knew exactly what she was doing when she'd donned the knee-length dress. The goal was to drive him crazy during the ceremony, the brunch after-ward, and on the way back to the hotel. She didn't expect to have an unwearable, expensive ass dress a mere minute after he'd stepped into the room, breakfast in hand.

Martin wrapped his arms around her from behind. Rubbing his nose over her ear, he kissed her there and whispered, "You know this is your fault, right?"

Ryleigh giggled. "It is not my fault that you're a horny bastard."

He slid a hand between her thighs, cupping her pussy in his palm. *Oh shit.* In her haste to take a second shower and figure out what to wear, she'd forgotten to put on a robe. Naked Ryleigh equaled Sexed Ryleigh in Martin Sullivan's book.

Gingerly, she eased out of his grasp and wrapped the sheet around her. Holding up a hand when he inched closer, she said, "Don't take another step, baby. As much as I would love to come again, we really need to get moving."

Martin smiled. Under normal circumstances, the wicked, delicious, make-her-wet smirk would have made her drop her sheet and let him have his way with her. But... *no.* Not now.

She shook her head. "How about you leave? Yes, go pick up Mama Lil and come back to get me."

Martin held up a hand, with her black lace bra hanging on his forefinger. "Come get it?"

Ryleigh couldn't help but smile. Since she'd reconnected with Martin, her desire for him had never waned. In fact, she was a thirsty beast for her hubby. Telling him no was akin to not eating Mama Lil's blueberry pancakes. But right now, she couldn't afford to get lost in his *fuck-me* hazel eyes or get wrapped in his strong arms.

She reached out and snatched the undergarment. Only he didn't let it go. The fun tug-of-war they played over her bra should have ended with another orgasm, but she couldn't do that to Ava. "Baby, please! Don't turn me into a bad godmother."

Laughing, Martin let her bra go but pulled her closer to him. "Okay." He brushed his lips over hers. "I'll go. We'll finish this tonight."

Ryleigh wrapped her arms around his shoulders and kissed him fully. "Tonight," she murmured against his lips. "Now, go. I'll be ready when you get back."

Forty minutes later, Ryleigh dashed into the Rosewood Heights Baptist Church, the same church she'd spent plenty of Sundays pretending to pay attention to extended hymns and long sermons.

When she approached the front of the church, she noticed the furious glare of Mother Parker, who'd always hated when people arrived late to the sanctuary. She also didn't miss the knowing glances and not-so-subtle smirks of her besties. Ava turned back, arching a brow and directing her to sit in the pew behind them.

Taking her seat next to Raven, she grumbled. "Don't say a word."

"I'm not saying anything." Raven giggled. "But Mother Parker looks like she's ready to get the switch."

Ryleigh glanced over at the gray-haired woman. She smiled at the older woman. "I wish she would. I will pull that old hat and that wig off with no hesitation." Mac laughed and covered it up with a cough, signaling she'd heard Ryleigh's quip. A chorus of "*shhhhs*" rang out in response.

Bishop Roberts stepped up to the podium and greeted everyone. He'd officiated most major events in town and today was no exception. At eighty-eight years old, the man still had a strong voice and an authoritative presence. Meaning, he could probably still put the fear of God himself into the kids of the church.

He gave honor to the Most High and acknowledged every single minister and deacon in the church. After his extended testimony, he launched into a "short" message about babies and the blessing of parenthood before he inappropriately told every wife to be good to her husband.

"This is so awkward," Raven mumbled.

It wasn't the first time the minister had said something

like this. During Ava's wedding, he'd thrown in something similar. "Tell me about it," Ryleigh whispered.

The Bishop mentioned how happy he was to be able to christen the newest Baby Prescott. He spoke about how he'd christened, baptized, and married every Prescott since 1965. The Prescott Family had sowed many seeds for the church over the years, from restoring the church roof's cross and donating turkeys for the Thanksgiving food drive every year to bankrolling the renovation and expansion of the building.

Ryleigh shifted in her seat, linking her hand with Martin's as the ceremony went on and on. *And on.* Finally, they were called to the front to make everything official. Ava had chosen all four ladies to be Owen Jr.'s godmothers, as she'd done with two-year-old Maddie. Once everyone was situated, the Bishop read the appropriate scriptures and said a bunch of prayers.

Baby "Sully" was passed between each godparent. The cutie pie smiled at most of them but cried when Mother Parker reached out to touch his forehead. *That's GMa's baby!* Unfortunately, Ryleigh was the only one that ended up with a glob of drool on her cheek. But it was worth it to get that wet kiss from her favorite godson. Another prayer later, they were finally done. And she was one step closer to a Mimosa. *About damn time.*

———

"Sheeiiiit, are we really talking about this?" Ryleigh sipped her third Mimosa. It was brunch so she felt she couldn't go harder than that. But the conversation had just taken a turn that definitely warranted something stronger than champagne. Tequila, Hennessey, Fireball.

The small, intimate reception at Rosewood Estates had

been amazing. The food was tasty, the dessert was delicious, and… *This Mimosa is almost gone.* Ryleigh scanned the room, looking for her wonderful hubby. The fellas must have been off somewhere talking golf or some other shit.

Pulling out her phone, she texted him a request for another drink.

"Y'all heffas can count me out." Mac took a long gulp of her drink.

Raven stood. "If we're going to do this, I need some fresh air."

Ryleigh sighed heavily. *This is some straight bullshit.* For real. There was no way in hell she'd agree to what Ava had just proposed. As if her bestie hadn't just popped out baby number two. As if her friend hadn't *also* screamed bloody murder during her worst contractions.

Quinn jumped up, nearly tipping over the table and all the drinks. Mac shouted while Ryleigh saved what was left of her drink and finished it off.

Ryleigh tuned Quinn out as she implored them to consider her proposed challenge. *I need to get out of here.*

"Quinn's right," Ava said. "We haven't discussed it in a long time."

Glaring at Ava, Ryleigh folded her arms across her chest. "That's because you won. Hence, the reason we're here."

Ava lifted her shoulders. "Don't kill the messenger."

Ryleigh absolutely wanted to kill Ava. Her friends continued their talk, but Ryleigh had more important things to worry about. She turned in her seat, meeting several gazes in the room in search of… *Where the hell is Martin with my drink?* When she turned back to her friends, Mac was gone.

Ryleigh blinked, scanning the immediate area for Mac. *Did I miss something?*

"Get your ass up," Raven murmured, pulling Ryleigh to her feet. "Come on."

"But my drink," Ryleigh whined.

Raven handed her two drinks. At this point, Ryleigh didn't even care where they'd come from. On their way out of the room, she ran into Martin, who held out the drink she'd asked for. She gave Raven one of the glasses back and took the one Martin gave her.

"Where are you going?" he asked.

Ryleigh kissed him. "If I'm not back in ten, come save me."

He laughed and swatted her behind. "Got it."

The warm June air felt like heaven to Ryleigh when she stepped out into the beautiful garden. The soft scent of peonies and roses wafted to her nose and she inhaled. "Smells so good," she murmured, before she sat on a bench. She sipped her drink. "So, listen, I think it's time we hang up the Best Friends Challenges. We're old as hell. It was fun when we were young and shit, but I'm done."

"I. Know." Raven crossed her legs.

Quinn didn't seem fazed by their objections, though. Instead, she brought up the last challenge and how happy they all were with how it turned out.

Shit, she's playing hardball. Ryleigh couldn't discount the benefit of the last challenge. But enough was enough.

Mac agreed that the wedding challenge changed all of their lives in a good way. "I'm not looking for anymore challenges."

Ava asked them to consider one more. "You ladies will love this one."

Once again, Ryleigh wondered how such a beautiful trip had turned into a nightmare. She texted Martin: *I thought I told you to come save me.*

A second later, Martin's reply came through: *I got you.*

"*Baby Bump Boot Camp!*" Ava shouted.

Ryleigh's gaze flashed to her bestie. "What the fuck are you talking about? What the hell is a *Baby Bump Boot Camp*? And why would that be something I'm interested in?"

Raven snickered. "You've been hanging around Quinn's crazy ass way too long."

Ryleigh expected Mac to chime in, to agree with her in just as many colorful, fun cuss words. But, no... Mac just stared ahead.

These heffas broke Mac.

That was okay, though. Ryleigh would speak for her. "Hell. No."

Raven joined in with her, letting them know she wasn't interested either.

"So why don't we hear her out?" Quinn asked, hope glimmering in her eyes. That ever-present hope her friend always had.

Nope. No sad doe eyes would convince her this was a good idea. Not at all.

"Just like we tuned your ass out when you initially mentioned this challenge to us, we plan on doing the same to her," Mac finally told Ava.

Ava paced in front of them, explaining the concept of a fuckin' baby bump boot camp. Ryleigh couldn't come up with a good enough reason to justify paying money for that shit. To get pregnant. Which wasn't something she ever wanted to do. *Again.*

But Ryleigh couldn't say that because no one knew that she'd already been there, done that. And barely lived to tell the tale.

Should I say something? she thought.

"I'll take the class," Mac said, pulling Ryleigh from her thoughts.

What the hell?

"But don't expect me to try and have a baby afterwards," Mac continued. "I can't commit to that."

Frowning, Ryleigh tried to make sense of Mac's reasoning as Raven grumbled about taking Best Friends Challenges too far, which Ryleigh agreed with wholeheartedly.

Before she could object again, though, Quinn added, "If you don't get pregnant within a year, the next girls trip is on you. And it won't be cheap!"

That damn Quinn. Her sweet friend with high hopes had latched on to Ava's bullshit idea and sprinted out the door. There would be no slowing this down now. At all. Quinn rambled on about babies and lives being better. And all Ryleigh could do was drink. If she was lucky, she'd get too drunk to remember this in the morning.

"Ryleigh?" Ava asked, her arm in the air holding a glass. "You in?"

Staring at each of her friends, she wanted to cuss every single last one of them out and run for the hills. But she was smart enough to know she wouldn't win the battle. So she made a decision. She'd agree to this stupid ass challenge and then purposefully lose. *That's it, that's all.* If she had to fork over thousands of dollars for a trip? *I'll do that shit.*

"Fine," she grumbled, raising her empty glass. "Mac?" Ryleigh elbowed Mac, who was once again staring ahead, a dazed look in her eyes.

After a little prodding, Mac finally raised her glass.

Strong hands massaged her shoulder and she jumped. Warm lips grazed her ear. "I'm here to save you?" Martin whispered.

"Too late," she grumbled, glaring at him. "Too damn late."

Baby Bump Boot Camp

"A baby pact?" Martin fell back on the mattress once they made it back to their suite at the Rosewood Inn.

Ryleigh kicked off her shoes and climbed onto the mattress. "Yes." She wrapped her arms around her hubby's waist. "Can you believe that?" She smiled when he cocooned her in his embrace.

The first thing she felt was comfort. The next thing she felt was acceptance. Ryleigh never wanted this feeling to end. She always wanted this ease between them, the silent understanding that he'd always given her. Even when he'd pursued her, he never pushed himself on her or tried to rush her into anything. And Ryleigh appreciated that. She hoped it would remain that way, but she couldn't be sure. Especially since she'd held on to such a huge secret for so many years.

He kissed her brow, and she melted into him. *God, I love him so much.*

"No, I can believe it," he said. "What I *can't* believe is that you agreed to it?"

"Right? Shocked the hell out of me, too. I do have a plan, though."

Martin leaned back, silently encouraging her to meet his gaze. When she did, he asked, "You have no intention of following through."

Ryleigh bit down on her bottom lip and nodded. "I don't want to get pregnant," she admitted. "I don't want to have a baby."

"Right now?" he asked softly.

Not ever. "No."

"That's…fair."

"Fair?"

He shrugged. "What else would it be? If you're not ready, you're not ready."

She swallowed past a hard lump in her throat. Because that look in her man's eyes, the piercing stare he was giving her right at this moment, looked a lot like disappointment —in her. *Or maybe even hurt?*

"We've never talked about this," he said. "But I always assumed we would one day."

While they were dating, they hadn't discussed kids. In the short time they'd been married, he'd never even voiced a desire to have a baby. Ryleigh had been blissfully okay with that. Now that they were in this precarious situation, with the new Best Friends Challenge time clock bearing down on them, she figured they should have had this discussion a long time ago. If he wanted kids, they had a big problem. Because she didn't.

Ryleigh had never been naïve. Her childhood didn't allow for much daydreaming or hoping for a fairytale ending. Martin had made it okay to revel in him, to love him with everything she had. But babies? The thought of being pregnant, of going through hours of hard labor, of long ass bouts of bedrest and a months-long maternity leave didn't appeal to her. She didn't want to uproot *her* life because her friends were ready to be mothers. She didn't need to have a horde of kids to feel good about herself. Play dates and baby showers didn't give her warm and fuzzy feelings. Just… No.

"Do you want kids, Ryleigh?" he asked.

Fear. It raced through her limbs and squeezed her heart. Now would be the time to tell him the truth, to tell him what she'd never told another living soul. But she couldn't bring herself to say it out loud. "I don't want to have a baby because of some pact," she said instead.

"You had a wedding because of a pact," he countered with a raise of his brow.

Ryleigh sat up, turning her back to him. "That's not what happened. I didn't marry you because of a pact, Martin."

"But there *was* a pact."

She dropped her gaze, focused on her toes against the blah-brown carpet. "A pact that I would have happily lost if we hadn't run into each other again. You know I've never done anything for any reason other than because I wanted to."

That was the honest truth. Ryleigh had survived an abusive, alcoholic mother because she wanted to, because she wanted better for her life. Everything she'd achieved in her life, she'd done through hard work and sheer willpower. She moved to Michigan because it was her dream to attend the University of Michigan. She became a mechanical engineer because she loved cars and enjoyed being an integral team member for one of the top three automotive companies in the country.

First kiss, first summer job, first sex, first wedding… Those little challenges with her friends were a way to bond with them. That awkward first time fuck she'd had with

Narvin Long way back when? It had nothing to do with the challenge, but everything to do with the fact that he was nice and she liked him. And Martin? *My beautiful, sexy husband.* Ryleigh married him because she fell so dangerously in love with him she couldn't imagine life without him. And because he'd asked her.

"So why agree to it?"

Ryleigh glanced back at him over her shoulder. "Because? I don't know. It's what we do."

"Ryleigh, you agreed to go to a *Baby Bump Boot Camp.* You raised your hand and said *we'd* participate."

"Yeah, I did." She stood up and turned to face him, hands on her hips. "But it's not like I implanted your seed in my vagina. It's a stupid baby spa or something. Less than a week of healthy eating, exercise, and sex talk. We're not walking out of there with an embryo in my womb."

Martin laughed. "Maybe not, but that's a lot of wasted time if you don't want to be pregnant right now. We could spend that time on a beach somewhere."

Ryleigh climbed back on the bed, but she didn't make a move to touch him again. Facing him on all-fours, she said, "I miss my friends. It's been a long time since we've hung out."

Shaking his head, he pulled her forward until she was on top of him. "You know I'll do anything for you, right?"

She nodded, tracing a finger over one of the buttons on his shirt. "I know."

For some reason, Ryleigh wanted to cry. Correction, she wanted to sob. Because she never questioned his loyalty, his willingness to do whatever she wanted. And before today, she would have unequivocally believed she'd do the same. But now… If he asked her to carry his child she wasn't sure she could say yes or even tell him *why* she'd made the decision.

"I won't say no," he said. "But I do feel like there's a bigger conversation that needs to be had."

Instead of speaking to that, she said, "I love you. I want you. I need you."

Martin's eyes softened. "I know. I also know when you're ready to stop talking. Take your clothes off." He brushed his lips against hers. "Now," he ordered, smacking her ass lightly.

Elated that he'd basically just agreed to drop the subject and fuck her, she struggled to stand up on the bed from her position. Ryleigh must have fallen on her butt three times. She wanted to look graceful and sexy, but *shit*, it was hard to stand up on a mattress. *Especially when I drank too much damn liquor and ate so many of those little cupcakes at the brunch.*

The soft sound of his chuckle let her know she probably looked like a complete and horny fool. But she finally made it to her feet. "Stop laughing at me."

"I'm sorry, baby." He grinned at her. "I love that you tried to stand up and everything, but there's a way to take your clothes off while laying down."

Giggling, she glanced down at him. "Oh shut up. I'm trying to be sexy here." It was the least he deserved since he was definitely going to deliver her another orgasm at the end of this.

Channeling her inner sexy beast, Ryleigh winked at him, flicked the top button of her dress open, and bared her shoulder for him.

He gripped her ankles as a wicked smile spread across his lips. "Slow."

"Slow?" she croaked.

"Did I stutter? Come closer. I want to see every inch of you."

Shit. The low rumble in his voice coupled with the

heat in his eyes, made her feel woozy. Desire coursed through every inch of her body and she ached with a need that only he could fulfill. Ryleigh didn't know if she had it in her to go slow. She wanted him inside her. Right now.

Yet, she did as she was told, slowly taking her dress off and throwing it behind her. Smirking, she pushed her panties down and used her foot to dangle the lacy material over his head.

Martin took the fabric and tossed it away before he beckoned her to him with his forefinger. "Where do you want me to touch you?"

Ryleigh bit down on her bottom lip. "Everywhere."

With a raised brow, he said, "Show me."

Letting out a strangled whimper, she once again did as she was told and slid her hands over the tops of her breasts, down her stomach, to her core.

Dark, hooded eyes met hers. "How do you want me to touch you?" he asked.

"Oh," she breathed, slipping her finger over her slick folds. "Like this."

Martin took his shirt off. "Do it," he ordered.

Once again, Ryleigh did as she was told, sucking in a deep breath when her finger brushed against her clit. His heated gaze felt like his caress on her sensitive skin. Martin hadn't touched her, but it felt like his hands were everywhere. On her breasts, on her stomach, on her pussy... "Oh god," she moaned. "Please."

"Keep going," he whispered as he pushed his pants and boxer briefs down, giving her a glimpse of his beautiful, hard dick. "Come for me so I can see it."

Closing her eyes, she massaged her clit with one finger while her other hand fondled her heavy breasts. When her orgasm crested within her, she dropped to her knees and fell back onto the mattress as she groaned his name over and over again.

She felt him over her, kissing his way up every inch of her body until his lips pressed against hers. "I love you so much, baby," he whispered.

Ryleigh kissed him. "I love you, too."

With their mouths fused together—licking, sucking, biting—he slid inside her, filling her completely. Hard and fast was Ryleigh's favorite and Martin always delivered. They raced to completion, giving and taking, pushing and pulling, until she cried out her release. When Martin followed, he growled out her name and collapsed on top of her.

"Damn," she whispered when she finally caught her breath. "That was so…"

Martin nipped her chin. "Fuckin' good," he finished for her. "But don't get too comfortable. Turn around." He placed a lingering kiss to her mouth. "I'm not done with you yet."

———

I'm going to bite Martin's damn finger off.

Ryleigh frowned at her husband, standing next to her holding up a carrot. The *Baby Bump Boot Camp* had already made her regret her decision to attend. In fact, she'd been in a perpetual state of pissed-off-ness since it had started.

Who the hell does fifty lunges in one damn day? Raven's ass, that was who. Exercise and the sound of her physically fit and overly competitive friend telling her to "push through" made day one un-freakin-bearable. Ryleigh was convinced that squats were evil and deserved to die a slow and painful death. And to make matters worse, they rounded out the intense day with a shitty walk around a track. Let's just say it didn't end well for Ryleigh. Instead of hot shower sex with Martin, she'd spent the night soaking in the Jacuzzi because her body felt like she'd been hit by a bus. *I hate working out.*

Day two was no better. Hours of mind-and-body wellness had fried Ryleigh's brain. And Zen with Quinn pretty much sucked because her friend couldn't stop smiling and talking during the various presentations. Ryleigh loved her friends. Really. She'd put her best foot forward to participate, with them and for them. But her hard limit on talk about essential oils was fifteen minutes. Even then, that was pushing her already frayed nerves. So, she'd bolted in the middle of a discussion about the use of carrier oils and the benefits of lavender and mandarin oils.

"Baby?" Martin waved the carrot in front of her face. "You're not paying attention."

"On purpose," she tossed back, adding in a hard eye roll for good measure.

Maybe the *Baby Bump Boot Camp* wouldn't be so bad if they didn't have to listen to their two personal coaches, Ricky and Philomena? *Okay, so either way it would have sucked.* But the simple fact that she had to look at them all day amplified her annoyance to the nth degree. Ricky with his frizzy hair and Philomena with her bright-and-never-matching outfits. *Ugh.*

Sighing, Ryleigh forced her attention to the front of the room. Today, the focus was healthy eating. It felt like a constant smack to her hand. The list of not-good-for-pregnant-women foods they'd spouted off was growing rapidly every second. No cold cuts. *Shit.* She loved turkey sandwiches. Throw out the Cocoa Puffs or Corn Pops for breakfast. Only fortified cereals like yucky Kashi. Forget about margaritas or cognac or Mimosas. Excess alcohol consumption was a no-no when trying to conceive.

The list of foods to eat made Ryleigh cringe. Martin loved fresh fish, so she'd gotten used to it over the years. But she absolutely hated anything that resembled a bean. No baked beans, no lima beans, no pinto beans. And red beans and rice? *Hell no.* Rice was one of God's greatest creations and didn't need to be sullied with beans.

"Why are you so happy?" she asked Martin.

He shrugged. "I'm actually not that happy. But you dragged me here. Why not make the best of it?"

"You know this is stupid."

Chuckling, he said, "I wouldn't call it stupid. It's actually good information."

"That you know we won't use. You love butter just as much as I do."

They'd already learned the dos and don'ts of cooking for conception and a subsequent pregnancy. Now, each couple had to prepare a nasty meal, with no butter and light seasoning.

For her part, Ryleigh loved butter and heavy seasonings. *Butter* was her friend. *Butter* had been a comfort during lonely and trying times. *Butter* made everything taste better —chicken, rice, grits, oatmeal, toast, vegetables. The fact that Ricky and Philomena had spent minutes turning *Butter* into the villain of their story, didn't sit right with her. She wanted to protest, but she'd refrained.

"I'm not arguing that fact," Martin muttered. "But you've been on one this whole week. This is *your* thing. You wanted to come here with your friends. And you've had an attitude since we got here."

"Because…" *What?* Ryleigh couldn't even finish her thought. He was completely correct. She'd been a raging bitch from the moment they'd arrived. Mac had called her on it last night and Ava had followed suit at breakfast that morning. "Never mind," she grunted.

"Baby, relax." Martin traced her lips with that ugly carrot. "It's going to be alright."

"Stop," she hissed, snatching it away from him. "You're enjoying this too much."

"Oh, I am." Martin grinned. "But you need to listen to the demonstration, at least. There's a prize for the best prepared meal. And because I know you can cook your beautiful ass off, I'm going to insist that you put forth the effort so we can win that shit."

Ryleigh sighed. "Fine. I'll pay attention, fry up this carrot, and pretend it's a healthier version of bacon. But I don't have to like it."

"Thanks, baby." He swatted her butt. "I know you'll knock it out."

"*You* just better knock *me* out tonight with at least two orgasms."

Martin winked at her. "I got you. No worries."

For her husband, Ryleigh became the star pupil. She substituted butter with Greek yogurt, rice with cauliflower and made a healthy, yet tasty, lunch that ultimately won the contest.

Martin kissed her cheek. "See I knew you could do it."

"Thanks for being a talented sous chef, baby. Now, we can say that we won the contest."

"Which is good. Since I know we're not going to win the actual challenge," he added under his breath.

Ryleigh swallowed hard. *The damn challenge.* They hadn't really discussed her actually getting pregnant after that first day. Martin had simply agreed to sign up for the camp and kept it moving. But the more they'd participated, the more she felt the foundation of their perfectly constructed life shift, the more she noticed the growing crack in their peace. A real conversation was in the cards for them, and she definitely wasn't looking forward to it. *At all.*

*ive months later*

Ryleigh's pussy hurt. Normally, she'd be elated or sated, because a vagina-ache almost always meant one thing—good, toe-curling sex. Today she couldn't say her crotch was sore because Martin had given her multiple orgasms, though. Shit, she'd be happy if she could come once. *That's a story for another day.* Unfortunately, floating on Cloud Climax wasn't her current state. Nope, Ryleigh was dead. Because spin class sucked.

Lawd! Everybody and their mama knew Ryleigh hated any form of exercise. In fact, she never understood why people invited her to walk, run, swim, or do yoga. Yet, she'd received an invite to join a new boutique gym and participate in an introductory class. On the surface, it was an innocent enough invitation. After all, the gym was owned by her good friend's younger brother and Ryleigh loved to support black-owned businesses. What she didn't expect? Dying a slow, tortuous death on a stationary bike.

Ryleigh had challenged herself in the mirror before she'd left home. Her goal was to rise to the occasion and do her damn thing in whatever class her friend Blake had signed her up to join. When she'd entered the gym an hour ago, she'd recited all types of affirmations in her head in an attempt to psych herself out. Even when she stepped into the room and noticed the bikes lined up, she'd thought, "*Easy peasy. I can ride a damn bike.*"

The tide turned quickly, though, highlighting the obvious fact that she was incredibly unprepared for this damn class and that devil bike. There was no chorus of "Eye of the Tiger" playing in her head. The only thing she heard was the old church hymn that said, "Lord, I need you to help me."

Instead of feeling invigorated, she felt like someone had literally stolen her breath. Instead of finishing her first class like a pro, she'd collapsed on the mat next to her bike. She might as well had been *the* mat. Because she couldn't move, she couldn't think, she couldn't even blink. The only thing she could do was stare at the gray ceiling.

"Girl!" Blake stared down at her, hands on her hips. "Are you okay?"

Ryleigh shook her head. "Your brother just killed me." She glared at Asa, who was leading the class. Long gone was the sweet, little boy she'd met years ago. In his place was the loud drill sergeant who'd seemingly taken pleasure from her pain.

Blake bent down. "Ry, if I have to pick your ass up, I'm going to record that shit and blast it on IG."

"I don't care," Ryleigh grunted. "You should probably call an ambulance. I really think I'm going to die on this floor." Her chest hurt, her arms shook, her gut throbbed, and her legs probably didn't work anymore.

Her friend grumbled a curse. "Give me your hand."

Ryleigh took Blake's hand and let her pull her to her feet. No small feat considering her friend weighed fifty pounds less than she did. But Blake Young was a black belt in karate and practically lived in the gym—when she wasn't coaching women on how to effectively break up with their dead weight boyfriends. Yes, that was a real job and her friend earned quite a living doing it.

"Thanks." Ryleigh shuffled over to a bench and plopped down.

Blake shook her head. "What the hell am I going to do with you? I've never seen you give up on anything."

That was true. Ryleigh was a professional finisher. She'd worked hard to get to where she was in her career and in her life. She'd sacrificed many things to climb her way out of the hellhole that was her life with her mother.

"Marrying Martin has made you soft," Blake sipped from her water bottle. "In-home sex does it every single time. First, you start waxing poetic about love. Then, you walk down that aisle and your insides turn to mush."

"Girl, stop. I'm not soft. But you know I hate working out."

"It's time to stop hating and start doing something. Aren't you supposed to be working on your baby bump right now?" Blake winked, then ducked in time to miss the flying towel Ryleigh sent her way. "Hey! Stop throwing shit."

"How about you stop *talking* shit?"

Blake stuck her tongue out. "Never!"

Rolling her eyes, Ryleigh added, "And get out of my business."

"You should have never told me about that challenge because you know I have lots of questions."

And Ryleigh had heard all of them, from "*What kind of crazy challenge is that?*" to "*How the hell is it going to work?*" to "*Are you going to call each other when you're ovulating?*" She'd yet to answer any of them, though.

"Girl, go finish spinning," Ryleigh said. "I'll be fine right here. Or out there." She pointed toward the door.

"Fine, I'll finish my workout. But it's been months and you still haven't spilled. I want to know what's going on with you."

So does everyone else, including Martin.

"I also want to know why your normally competitive self isn't pregnant yet," Blake added.

Raven and Quinn had already announced their pregnancies, and Ryleigh was excited for her besties. She still had no desire to join them. In fact, she'd already contacted a travel agent about booking the next girls trip on her dime. And she would attend every baby shower and kiddie birthday party with a mound of gifts and a pint of cognac for her nerves.

"You obviously don't know me as well you think you do," Ryleigh muttered.

Blake pointed at her. "I heard that."

"So? Did I stutter?" Ryleigh blew her friend a kiss. "Now, go on back to that death trap masquerading as a bike."

Ryleigh waited a few minutes before she stood and left the exercise room. She stopped and bought a smoothie from a little kiosk and ventured over to the cafe seating area. She was engrossed in a game on her phone when Blake slid into the chair across from her.

"Class over already?" Ryleigh asked.

"Yeah. I told Asa he needed to extend it a little."

Ryleigh frowned. "Stop trying to tell your brother what to do. This is his business."

Blake shrugged. "I'm older than him, so I can give him a few pointers."

"I'm older than you, but your ass is always trying to tell me what to do."

They'd met when Ryleigh was the Resident Assistant at her college dorm. Blake was a freshman but had impressed Ryleigh with her aversion to college bullshit. Bonding over their mutual dislike of stupid people and general willingness to whoop someone's ass, they'd become fast friends and had remained close through the years.

With Ryleigh's besties living in various cities across the nation, it was so good to have a friend in town. And since Blake had a slew of siblings, Ryleigh had a nice extended family away from family.

Blake sipped her own smoothie, before slamming the cup down on the table. "Forget this shit. I need a drink. Let's grab some food."

Within an hour, they were seated at Ryleigh's favorite restaurant, *Carrabba's Italian Grill*. After she took a sip of her blackberry sangria, she moaned. "So damn good. This hit the spot."

Blake grinned, and clinked her glass against Ryleigh's. "This shit is the bomb."

They chatted for a few minutes about work. For her part, Ryleigh didn't have anything new to report. She loved her job as a program manager for one of the Big Three automotive companies in the Metro Detroit area. Two weeks ago, she'd returned from a three-month assignment in Kentucky—to an empty house. Because Martin had thrown himself into a new project, one that required *him* to be away for a while. Usually, she'd be holed up at her house naked with Martin after such a long time apart. But… *Yeah, that's another story for another day.*

"What about you?" Ryleigh asked. "How's business?"

"Girl, booming!" Blake's official title was Clinical Psychologist, like her famous parents and several of her siblings. But she'd carved out a nice niche for herself as the Breakup Expert. "I've been doing a lot of press, even been approached to write a damn book."

Recently, Blake had written an article titled "It's Not Me, It's You" basically flipping the break-up line "it's not you, it's me" on its head. The three-minute read challenged women —and some men—to stop lying to people when breaking up and quit taking all the blame in the deterioration of a relationship. The shit went viral in under two hours. Women from all around were sharing it, discussing it in group chats, and sending it to their boyfriends or ex-boyfriends.

Ryleigh gave her a high five. "That's awesome. Are you thinking about doing it?"

Blake shook her head and waved a dismissive hand. "Ain't nobody got time for that shit."

Laughing, Ryleigh shook her head. "Girl, you need to stop. What else are you doing?"

"Trying to keep myself out of trouble. My last sex shit-uation nearly made me throw in the towel."

Frowning, Ryleigh said, "Wait, I thought you liked Colton."

With a roll of her eyes, Blake downed the rest of her drink. "Hell. No. His ass is a stalker. Everywhere I turn, he's breathing down my damn neck, acting like a piece of Velcro. And Mom damn near had a happy heart attack when he showed up at the family barbecue, looking like a corny bastard with flowers and that annoying grin he's always sporting. You know she loved the soap opera coincidence, right? I should have known he'd be ridiculous with a name like Colton."

Ryleigh cracked up. Blake and her six siblings were all named after characters from various soap operas. "I bet Mama Vic was grinning from ear-to-ear. What made you even invite him to your parents' house? That's not even like you."

"It was the dick."

Ryleigh choked on her drink and patted her chest. Her blunt friend had never had a filter. Reminded her of herself and Mac. "Warn a sista next time, please."

"What?" Blake shrugged. "I'm telling the truth. He's so damn talented, I almost lost my mind. *Almost.* I had to shake myself out of the dick trance so I could look at everything objectively for a moment. But, ooh Lawd... his fuck game was stellar."

Ryleigh glanced at the two women seated at a table next to their booth, who were now laughing at Blake fanning herself exaggeratedly. No doubt they'd just heard the latest chapter in The World According to Blake.

"I always tell my clients not to let good dick keep you in a trash relationship," Blake continued. "What do I look like staying with Corny Colton because he knew how to work that thang? A happy pussy doesn't necessarily translate to a happy life."

"Girl, don't I know it," Ryleigh agreed.

Blake held up a hand. "Wait a minute."

Oh shit. Ryleigh had messed up.

"What the fuck are you agreeing with me for?"

Luckily for Ryleigh, the ladies at the adjacent table stood and approached them. One of them asked Blake, "Aren't you The Breakup Expert?"

Blake flashed her patented *get-the-hell-out-of-my-personal-*

space-before-I-give-you-this-throat-punch smile and nodded. "I am."

The other lady clapped. "I shared your article with my ex and told him to kick rocks. It was the best thing I've ever done."

"Good. Glad I can help." Blake pulled out two business cards and handed one to each of the ladies. After a short exchange and a bit of advice, Blake waved at them as they walked out of the restaurant.

"That was nice of you to talk to them," Ryleigh said.

"Girl, I almost said something mean. You know I hate when strangers get in my space."

Ryleigh giggled. "I know," she agreed. "I'm glad you refrained from telling them off. Obviously, that one girl needed to talk."

It hadn't been lost on Ryleigh that the shorter of the two women was on the verge of tears before Blake took control of the conversation and told the lady to call her tomorrow morning.

"Right?" Blake shook her head. "I can tell she's going to be a lot of work."

The waitress arrived with their food and they started eating. Ryleigh was glad she'd braved the spinning class to get some quality time with Blake. She'd needed some laughter in her life.

"Don't think I forgot about your little slip earlier," Blake said. "What's going on, Ry?"

Ryleigh sighed. "Nothing. I was speaking about past relationships. Not Martin." It wasn't really a lie. It just wasn't the entire truth. Because at the moment, Ryleigh didn't have a happy pussy *or* a happy life.

It had been months since she'd made love to her husband. Granted, she'd been away for a while, but still... It wasn't uncommon for either of them to travel for work.

They'd always made it a point to stay connected, through impromptu or planned weekend visits, video chats, phone calls, or simple good morning and goodnight texts. But they'd barely spoken. His arms didn't feel like her personal warm cocoon anymore and his smile never reached his eyes.

Ryleigh wished she could blame the baby challenge. But she knew why things had spiraled out of control. And it wasn't the challenge or Martin. It was her. B*ecause I'm a freakin' coward.*

"Lies," Blake murmured. "I'm not going to push you. I *am* going to put on my serious face and encourage you to talk to Martin. I know you, and I know that you have a penchant of avoiding things to protect your peace. But I can see that whatever you're doing is not working."

Ryleigh felt the familiar burn of tears in her eyes. "We're just busy. It's been a long time since we've spent time together."

"Lying to me is one thing, but don't lie to yourself, Ry." Blake set her fork down and let out a heavy sigh. "I talk a lot of shit, all the time. But I'm going to say something. You don't have to answer. Just know that you can talk to me when you're ready."

Swallowing, Ryleigh said, "Go ahead."

"It's the baby challenge, isn't it?"

After a moment of silence, Ryleigh nodded.

"Let me guess, he wants a baby?"

Again, Ryleigh nodded.

"And you don't," Blake said.

"No," Ryleigh answered. "I don't."

Blake reached across the table and squeezed Ryleigh's hands. "Ry, you've never told me why you don't want to have kids."

Ryleigh had kept that secret close to her vest. She'd

never even told Mama Lil, let alone her besties. The only reason Blake knew she didn't want to have kids at all was because she'd let it slip during a drunken girls night out.

"I can't even begin to understand what's at play in your marriage," Blake said. "That's not my place. But you have to talk to Martin. You have to tell him your reasons why. You can keep it from everyone else, *except* him. He's your husband. You love him. I'd hate to see this tear you apart."

Dropping her gaze, Ryleigh sucked in a slow breath. "I do love him," she admitted softly. "I want to talk to him, but I feel like he won't understand."

"You're not giving him a chance, sweetie."

"I know. It's just hard. I can't seem to force myself to…" Ryleigh let out a frustrated sob, before she wiped a tear from her cheek. "Forget it. I'll figure it out."

"I'm actually starting to worry about you," Blake admitted. "Is it your health? Did something happen to you that affected your ability to have children?"

"No. It's nothing like that." Steeling herself, she looked at Blake. "You're right, I'll talk to Martin. We definitely can't go on like this."

Later, Ryleigh opened her front door. The living room was still, no sign of life. *No Martin.* With a heavy sigh, she kicked her shoes off and padded to the bedroom. Checking behind her—*as if anyone is here*—she hurried to the bedside table. Opening the drawer, she pulled out a bag of mini Snickers and immediately ate three of them. *So good.*

"Ry."

Ryleigh jumped, dropping the candy bars onto the floor. *Martin.* Their eyes met. *He looks so damn good.*

He stepped into the room. "Hey."

She tossed him a lame wave. "Hey," she murmured around a mouth full of milk chocolate, caramel, peanuts, and nougat. Once she successfully chewed her sweet treat, she said, "Hi. I didn't know you were coming home today." *Or at all.*

"Yeah." Martin inched closer to her but stopped a least a foot away from her. *Too far.*

Ryleigh stepped forward. "Baby, I—"

Martin held up a hand. "Ryleigh, wait."

She froze, clenching her hands into fists to keep herself from touching him. She'd missed him. "Martin, can—?"

"We need to talk. Now."

Chapter 2

*M*artin had warred with himself every minute of every day, for the past five months. He'd asked himself all of the questions, but never came up with answers that made things better. He'd made all the excuses, but they weren't good enough. Bottom line, he needed to talk to his wife. Because if they didn't have a real conversation soon, they wouldn't make it another day.

"You want to talk?" Ryleigh whispered.

"Don't you think it's time?" They'd been skating around each other for months, avoiding the inevitable conversation. Martin felt worse with each passing day. "It's been long enough."

Ryleigh nodded. "You're right."

No matter how angry he was with Ryleigh, he still loved her. *She's so damn beautiful and sexy.* And he'd missed her. He'd missed holding her, talking to her, loving her. Dressed in a pair of joggers and a t-shirt, she looked like an angel bathed in gold. Everything about her called to him, from her short hair to her brown eyes to those damn hips.

Martin studied her face, noted the light sheen of sweat on her brow and the tears brimming in her eyes. He hated to see her cry, but he had a feeling they'd both shed a few tears before the night was over.

"We can't go on like this," he said.

"Are you going to leave me?" she asked.

He blinked. "Why would you ask me that?"

Ryleigh's chin trembled. "Because you're so angry with me. Look at you! You're tense, stiff. We haven't talked, we haven't eaten dinner together, we haven't touched each other."

"Why do you think that is?"

"I'm guessing it's because of the baby pact."

"You're guessing?" he challenged.

The Best Friends Challenge wasn't the cause of the rift between them, but it was the impetus that had forced him to actually pay attention. That's when he noticed it—the haunted look in her eyes, the things she hadn't said, the assurances she'd never given. Since then, he'd allowed his doubts to creep in. Doubt had turned to disappointment. Disappointment had turned to anger.

Shrugging, she said, "What else could it be? Things haven't been right between us since then. Something between us has shifted, broken."

"No, not *something*. I can tell you exactly what's wrong with us. And you can, too."

Martin dreamed about her, spent nights obsessing about her body and her mind. He'd spent hours memorizing her quirks, familiarizing himself with her past, planning their future. He thought he knew her inside and out. But the last several months had made one thing very clear. *I don't.*

After years of marriage, countless moments with her, Martin felt uncertain about his wife and that didn't sit well with him. He loved Ryleigh beyond reason, but more than ever, she seemed like a stranger to him.

The realization that there was a part of her he'd never known, that there was a piece of her that she'd willingly kept from him, nearly destroyed him. Because he'd given her everything, all of this thoughts, his fears, his love.

Ryleigh grabbed his arm. "I shouldn't have agreed to the challenge without talking to you first. I know that now."

He backed away from her, effectively severing the contact. "Don't do that."

"Do what?"

"Make this about the damn challenge, Ryleigh!" he blared. "This is bigger than some pact with your friends!"

"Okay." She smacked her hands against her thighs. "What do think this is about?"

Martin snickered. "There you go again."

"What?" she shouted. "I'm trying to understand. I want to fix this."

"I don't believe you."

"Why?"

"The *Baby Bump Boot Camp* was five months ago, Ryleigh. We agreed we would table the discussion for later. It's way past *later*, and you haven't mentioned it at all. And I waited for you…to talk, to let me in, to say anything about it."

"Okay, but we're talking now."

"I shouldn't have to beg you to talk to me!"

"Martin, please?" Ryleigh stepped closer. "Don't be like this, don't be mad."

"The fact that you couldn't even give me the courtesy of a simple conversation, pisses me the fuck off. Five damn months. Why shouldn't I be mad? When I married you, I thought I was marrying someone who wanted to be in a relationship with me."

"What does that even mean?" Ryleigh said. "Of course, I want to be with you."

"Do you? Ryleigh, you keep talking but you're not saying anything. At this point, I feel like you're purposely missing the damn point." He paced away from her, hoping a little distance would ease his temper. Turning to her, he said, "I look at you and all I see is everything you're not telling me. All I feel is the loss of something I thought was beautiful—and solid. What is it going to take for you to tell me why you don't want to have my kid?"

Ryleigh gasped, stumbling back a step. She sat down on the bed. "Martin," she whispered.

"Just tell me," he pleaded, swallowing past a hard lump in his throat. "Just say it. I've never forced you to do anything. All I've ever asked is for you to be honest with me. If you can't me tell the truth, what do we have? What is salvageable here?"

"Everything, Martin." Ryleigh stood and approached him. Grabbing his hand, she said, "Everything."

He rested his forehead against hers. "You have to mean it."

"I do." She brushed her lips over his jaw. "I don't want to lose you." Ryleigh kissed him.

Even though he knew he shouldn't, he let her. It had been a long time since he was this close to her, since he'd felt her soft lips against his. She tasted like chocolate and tears, smelled like pears and green tea. And he loved it. "Baby," he murmured against her mouth.

Ryleigh trailed her fingers over his cheeks and held him to her. "Martin, please. I need you."

Martin wanted to pull her closer, strip her bare, and make love to her until the doubt subsided. Inevitably morning would come, though, and their problems would be waiting for them.

Reluctantly, he wrapped his hands around hers and gently pulled them from his face. "I can't. Not now." A tear fell from her eyes, and he wiped it away. "It won't help. Trust me."

"I know." She nodded. "This is just hard."

"Why, Ryleigh? Why can't you just talk to me?"

Averting her gaze, she backed away from him. "I'm scared."

"*Of me?*"

She shook her head. "Of the truth."

Martin should be upset that she'd finally admitted she'd been hiding something from him all along. All he felt was relief, like balm over dry skin. Because maybe they could finally move forward.

"I worry that you'll look at me differently once I tell you."

He searched her eyes. "Ryleigh, did you murder someone? Steal from the elderly? Vote for the current president?"

Frowning, she said, "No."

"Okay, then. There's nothing you can tell me that will make me love you any less."

"Can we go into the kitchen? I'd like to get something to drink before we talk."

Nodding, he followed her into the kitchen. Martin sat down while Ryleigh pulled out two glasses and poured them both a healthy shot of cognac. A moment later, she was seated in front of him.

Ryleigh took a sip. "During my freshman year in college, I worked for my professor as part of a work-study agreement."

Martin knew about this. He'd even met Professor

Jeffrey Marks and his family a couple of years ago, at an event.

"You know that already," Ryleigh added. "He was so good to me, Martin. There were times I didn't know if I would make it without Mama Lil, without my girls. But he and his wife welcomed me into their home, they treated me like I was their goddaughter."

His mind flitted ahead, imagining various scenarios. The first one? *Did Ryleigh have an affair with her professor?*

"Holly had struggled for years to conceive." Ryleigh finished her drink and set it on the table. "They spent thousands on it, going to specialists, harvesting eggs, having procedures. Ultimately, though, none of their efforts worked.

One day, they mentioned finding a surrogate and I applauded them. They interviewed candidates and settled on this woman from Muskegon, Michigan." Ryleigh shifted in her seat. "They hired attorneys, spent hours going over the contracts, paid the surrogate a lot of money. … The woman bailed right before the insemination. Holly cried for days after that."

Martin watched his wife intently, waiting for her to finish the story.

"This went on for years," Ryleigh continued. "I'd watched them deal with so much heartache and pain. Finally, I offered to be their surrogate."

He wasn't sure what he'd expected, but that wasn't it. "What?"

With a heavy sigh, Ryleigh continued her story. "I had to wait until my twenty-first birthday, but I carried *their* baby for them. I went through nineteen hours of labor before I delivered *their* baby. Then, I handed *their* beautiful baby girl over to her real parents and never spoke about it again."

"That's huge, Ry."

Ryleigh had maintained close contact with the Marks family. Hell, Martin spent time with them. He'd golfed with the professor, grilled steaks for their family, played softball with little Hailey. The entire time, he'd never suspected his wife had carried the spunky tween. And he didn't know what to feel about it or how to react. She'd hidden such a big part of her life from him. At the same time, she'd done something so selfless for someone else.

"It is," she agreed. "But I look at Hailey and I feel happy that I was able to give her to them. They're wonderful parents and they love her so much."

"I can understand wanting to help someone you love."

"Of course, I wanted to help." She averted her gaze, tracing the edge of the table with her thumb. "I wanted them to experience parenthood." She met his waiting gaze again. "I also did it because I needed the money."

"I thought Ava's parents paid for your tuition?"

"They did, but there were other expenses and my financial aid didn't cover them all. By my fourth year, I had racked up a significant amount of debt."

"What about your scholarship?"

"It barely covered room and board the first year. Rent in Ann Arbor is expensive. I knew I needed to go to grad school. And I didn't want to ask anyone else for help."

Martin was well aware of the challenges Ryleigh had faced in her life. Her mother had never helped her and Mama Lil wasn't wealthy. He also knew she hated to ask anyone for anything.

"There was no way I'd be where I am financially if I'd graduated with all those student loans, if I hadn't been able to use the money to pay for my master's degree," she explained. "But I would have done it for free because I love them that much."

Martin tried to process everything she'd just told him. He wondered how her experience translated to their current predicament. "Finish telling me."

"What else do you want to know?"

"All of it." He finished his drink. "Did you tell anyone?"

She shook her head. "No, I didn't. We planned it so that I'd deliver once the winter semester was over. I was lucky I got pregnant on the first try. I had the baby on May 29th." Ryleigh giggled. "I told everyone I had internship in London. I hid the pregnancy with big clothes and books, just like on TV. I made sure I stayed away from the girls and Mama Lil. Blake didn't know either."

"Did you have a non-disclosure agreement or something?"

"Not really," she replied. "I agreed not to shout it from the rooftops, but they never expected me to keep it quiet forever. That was my decision."

"I get it. It's not something you should broadcast to everyone. But I'm your husband. Why didn't you tell *me*?" At the very least, she should have mentioned it before they walked down the aisle.

"I don't know. I didn't want you to look at me the way you're looking at me now."

Martin knew that he felt some type of way, but he hadn't realized that he'd let those conflicted emotions bleed onto his expression. "Ryleigh, still…"

"I know. I should've told you. I wanted to tell you, but I just couldn't bring myself to say the words."

"What does this have to do with us and the baby challenge?"

"A lot. That pregnancy… I didn't have an easy time. I ended up with preeclampsia, on bed rest for three weeks.

After I had the baby, there were more complications. I don't want to go through that again."

"So this is not a matter of timing." The ache in the back of his throat intensified making it difficult to swallow. Earlier he wondered what her truth had to do with them. In his heart, he knew the answer. And it changed everything. "You never want to have another baby."

"No," she confessed. "I don't."

Martin couldn't really blame Ryleigh. Not really. They'd married without even talking about kids. He'd assumed they'd eventually have a baby. It had never occurred to him that they might not, that she didn't even want to have his kid.

Ryleigh squeezed his hand. "Baby, I was scared during the entire pregnancy. I'd heard the horror stories, watched the reality shows, and pretty much cried my way through all three trimesters. And I was young then. I'm older now. What if there are more complications? What if I have to be on bed rest for three months instead of three weeks? I can't do it. I can't put myself through that again."

He'd heard her reasons. He even understood them. But… "What about what I want?"

"You want a baby?"

Before the damn challenge, a baby had been the furthest thing from his mind. Martin had never done anything because others were doing it. When Owen and Ava started popping out babies, Martin had cheered them on. When Carter had announced that he and Brooklyn were expecting, he'd happily stepped in to be the godfather.

Having his own child had always been a far-off dream. At this point in their lives, they were committed to their careers and to their relationship. Now… "I do want to have a kid," he admitted. "I want you to be the mother of my child."

Tears spilled from her eyes and he fought against his instinct to comfort her. "I don't want to have a baby, Martin. I don't know if that will change anytime soon. Or ever."

Hearing the words out loud didn't make it better. It only made it worse. What could he say, though? Lashing out would change nothing, begging her wasn't going to happen. It was her body, her decision. Martin didn't like it, though. But he had no choice but to accept it if he wanted to be with her.

"Okay." The word sounded hollow to his own ears, like defeat.

"So what do we do?"

"What can we do?" Five months ago, their future seemed bright, promising. Now, they were in a sort of strange limbo. A crossroad that seemed daunting and almost insurmountable, and he didn't know how to fix it. "Listen, I think it's beautiful what you did for Jeffrey and Holly. Hailey is a healthy and happy little girl."

"But?" she prodded.

"I can't reconcile that selfless act with how selfish you've been with me. We could've discussed this a long time ago. We could have worked through this long before now. But you didn't trust me with your truth."

Ryleigh folded her arms across her chest. "If I had told you then, would it have changed your reaction?"

"Maybe. I don't know. If you'd told me then, these last five months might not have been so painful for us, though."

"Do you think we can work on this, compromise?"

"What is there to compromise on?" Martin stood. The contrast between the all-consuming love he felt for her mixed with the overwhelming anguish that continued to expand inside him made him feel unhinged. He needed some time away from her. He needed some time to think about everything. "You kept a major part of your life from me. You would have continued to stay silent had this challenge never happened. It's a lot to process, especially since the decision you made then affects our life now."

"You told me there was nothing I could do to stop you from loving me."

Martin sighed. "I haven't stopped loving you, Ryleigh." The burn of tears in his own eyes caught him off guard. "I love you so much. Sometimes it feels like I love you *too* much. Damn, I want to be okay with this, I want to be okay with your decision. I want you."

This much needed conversation confirmed that he'd married an extraordinary woman. Ryleigh had transformed her life to have a baby for another couple. His wife made a huge sacrifice for someone else because of her capacity to love. He should feel proud of her. *And I am.* Pride was just one of the many emotions fighting for dominance in his brain. But the hurt that he felt was winning the war. Because even though she'd made such a huge sacrifice for Jeffrey and Holly, she'd basically admitted that she wouldn't do the same for him.

"I need to go," he told her.

She grabbed his hand. "Wait, please. Don't go."

"Ryleigh, I can't stay here right now. I need time."

"Where are you going?"

Instead of answering her, he kissed her brow. "I'll call you in the morning." If he stayed there, he might say something he regretted. If he stayed there, he might have to accept that their relationship couldn't be salvaged if they wanted different things. If he stayed there, it might be the end of them.

Chapter 3

"Ry-girl, what are you doing here?" Mama Lil held out her arms and Ryleigh stepped right into them.

Damn, she needed that hug. She needed it so much that she'd hopped on a plane and flew her black ass all the way to Rosewood Heights. "I missed you," Ryleigh murmured against Mama Lil's shoulder.

Yes, she was in the middle of *The Little Rose*. Yes, she realized it was the busiest time of the day—breakfast. Yes, she was pretty sure that the townspeople in the dining room were watching her and ready to broadcast her sudden arrival to the entire Rosewood Heights community. *Word travels fast.* But she couldn't bring herself to let go of the woman that had been a mother to her when her own mother couldn't be bothered. Mama Lil had nurtured her, comforted her, and loved her through everything in her life. And she needed that warmth, that peace, that steadfast support right now.

Mama Lil pulled back and tilted her head. "Ry-girl?"

She rubbed Ryleigh's cheeks, dashed a fallen tear from her cheek. "Come on, chile. Let's get you something to eat."

A little while later, Ryleigh was cutting into a heaping mound of blueberry pancakes and taking her first bite. *Heaven with heavy syrup and a lot of butter.* "Thanks for this, Mama Lil."

"Anytime, baby." Mama Lil leaned forward. "Now, tell me what I want to know, girl. What brings you here so close to the holiday? Don't get me wrong, I'm happy to see your beautiful face. But you can't be surprising me like this. Makes me think something's wrong."

"I told you… I missed you."

"When you were young, I always knew when something was wrong with you. Your eyes give it away every single time. And I don't like that look in your eyes right now. Where's Martin?"

With a heavy sigh, Ryleigh set her fork down. "He's in Wellspring."

Martin's business partner, Carter Marshall, had moved to Wellspring, Michigan years ago to spearhead a project for their software company. While there, the widower met and fell in love with Brooklyn Wells. They married a short time later and had recently had a baby boy.

"This early?" Mama Lil pushed the jelly container to its rightful spot on the table and turned the sweetener holder clockwise. "I thought you two were going there for the holiday. Together."

"We are." Ryleigh took a sip of coffee. "He had business," she lied. Ryleigh knew Martin wasn't in Wellspring for work. He was in Wellspring because he needed to be away from *her*. It had been two days since she'd confessed the surrogacy to him. It had been two days since she'd broken his heart by telling him she didn't want to have his baby. It had been the hardest two days of her life.

"Business, huh?" Mama Lil raised a bow. "Is that so?"

Ryleigh cowered under Mama Lil's intense stare. The woman had super powers, able to read minds with a single glance. No sense in prolonging the inevitable. She'd come to Rosewood Heights to talk. Moving her fork around her plate, she said, "Mama Lil, I don't know what to do."

Frowning, Mama Lil asked, "Do about what?"

"Things are tense between us." Talk about understatement of the year. Tense would describe an argument about whether the toilet paper should go over or under. Tense was finding out that your spouse preferred cole slaw with his chitterlings or hated hot sauce on collard greens.

"Ryleigh, tell me."

She blinked, jarred by Mama Lil's serious tone and use of her full name. "Um, I... I can't," she stammered, gripping her suddenly sore throat. Taking a deep breath, she dropped her head. "We made a baby—?"

"Oh my!" Ryleigh met Mama Lil's eyes just in time to see tears spill from her eyes. "Oh my goodness," the older woman said, placed a hand over her mouth. "Are you pregnant? I have to tell Mary. And Ruby will be so excited to make the baby shower cake. Oh, and you better not name the baby one of those names that I can't pronounce. If you do, I'll be forced to call it 'baby' forever. Please don't disappoint me with that."

Ryleigh stared at Mama Lil. *What the hell?* "Mama Lil?"

"I think we should have your baby shower somewhere other than that highfalutin Rosewood Estates. I think it should be intimate, not ritzy." She nodded her head. "Yes. I can cater. And it will be nice and simple."

"Mama Lil," Ryleigh repeated.

"I'm sure Ava and her mother will try and take over, but I'm going to put my foot down on this. I have to get a

25

pad of paper so I can jot down these notes. You know I'll forget."

Mama Lil started to stand, but Ryleigh placed a hand on top of hers to stop her. "Mama Lil, stop."

With a deep frown on her face, Mama Lil sat back. "What's wrong? This is an exciting time for you and Martin." She pushed the plate of pancakes closer. "And you need to eat. Have you been resting? Is that why you have bags under your eyes? Are you nauseous? I have saltines in the back. I also shipped in that Vernors soda you love from Michigan."

"I'm not pregnant!" Ryleigh shouted. Embarrassed at her outburst, she glanced back and noticed several pairs of eyes on her. Sighing, she whispered, "Please stop planning my baby shower."

Mama Lil leaned forward, concern in her brown eyes. "Oh. Well, you've successfully confused the hell out of me this morning. First, with your sudden arrival. Then, with the baby mention. So why don't you just go ahead and talk?"

"Thank you." Ryleigh shifted in her seat. She stared at the blueberry pancakes. Any other day, she'd eat and talk. Now, she didn't really have an appetite. Pushing the plate away, she peered up at Mama Lil. "Only one of us wants a baby, Mama Lil."

"Oh."

"Back in June, the girls and I did a Best Fiends Challenge." Ryleigh explained the baby pact quickly, keeping it brief but concise. "Of course, I told Martin about it. He told me that he's okay with waiting, but…" She dropped her napkin on the table. "I don't want to wait. I just don't want a baby."

Mama Lil whistled. "That's a lot to take in."

"Tell me about it," Ryleigh murmured.

"I would ask why, but I think I know," Mama Lil said.

"Trust me, you don't know." Ryleigh steeled herself for the upcoming conversation. "I—"

"You don't want a baby because you already had one."

Ryleigh gasped. "Mama Lil? What? How do you…?"

Mama Lil smiled sadly. "Girl, you know you can't put anything past me. I knew you were pregnant the minute I saw you during your Christmas break that year. Those oversized sweatshirts didn't fool me." She chuckled softly. "And that story about an internship in London? Girl, please. Who do you think I am? Mama Gullible?"

Ryleigh laughed then. "Mama Lil, I love you so much."

"I love you, too. Now, tell me the rest."

Over the next twenty minutes, Ryleigh told Mama Lil about the surrogacy and the birth of Hailey. Then, she segued into the argument she had with Martin."

"It's like we've been living our lives walking on egg shells around each other," Ryleigh said. "Talking, but not saying anything. Hearing, but not listening. The other night, things intensified. We… I hurt him. That was never my intention. Now, I can't take it back. The damage is done."

"Ry-girl, now is not the time to throw in the towel."

"How can I fix this?"

"You can start by examining this fear of having a baby and recognizing it for what it really is."

Ryleigh pondered what Mama Lil said. She'd never really tried to analyze her reasons because they seemed pretty straightforward to her. Pregnancy was tough and she was a big crybaby who didn't want to go through it all again. Simple.

Mama Lil squeezed her wrist. "You're not your mother. Martin is not your father."

"I know that, Mama Lil." Ryleigh wasn't an idiot. She

didn't have the best childhood, but she'd never assumed she was anything like Harriett Fields. And Martin was a far superior man than her father had ever been. "This isn't about my mother."

"I think it is," Mama Lil said. "For so many reasons that you've yet to face. I've also watched you run from love your entire life." Ryleigh opened her mouth to respond, but Mama Lil held up a hand. "Let me finish."

Ryleigh clamped her mouth shut.

"Yes, you've let a few people in like me, your friends, and Martin. However, there's a part of you that has resisted love—giving it *and* receiving it. I know that's because of your mother. Having a baby for your mentor and his wife was selfless and proves that you have a big heart. But it was a task that you had to complete, a business transaction. Safe. Having your own baby, though, is not safe."

Damn it. Mama Lil might be on to something. Still, Ryleigh wasn't ready to consider the weight of that revelation. "The pregnancy was hard," she said.

Suddenly, she felt like something was sitting on her chest. She couldn't breathe, she couldn't think. *I have to get out of here.* Jumping to her feet, she bolted out of the restaurant. The balmy November weather outside didn't help either. Ryleigh felt hot, like she could keel over at any minute. Leaning against the wall of the building, she took in a few deep breaths and willed her heartrate to slow down.

A moment later, she heard the bell above the door and knew without a doubt it was Mama Lil. But she didn't turn around to face her. She couldn't look into those knowing eyes. A sob broke through and the dam broke.

Two strong arms wrapped around her from the back, followed by the calming voice that had soothed so many of her fears over the years. "Ry-girl, I love you." Mama Lil's voice was a shaky whisper, like she was crying, too. "I want you to have everything you've ever wanted; all the happiness you can stand. But I'm worried that you are going to let that man slip through your fingers if you don't stop carrying your mother on your back." Mama Lil turned Ryleigh in her arms and framed her face with her hands. "You are not Harriett Fields. You will be able to love any child you have with all of your heart. And it won't break you."

"I could have died," Ryleigh insisted lamely, still not willing to give in to the truth. "I don't want to do it again."

"Baby, don't. Stop lying to yourself. It's not a good look."

Ryleigh shook her head. "What if I fail at this? What if I can't handle being a mother?"

"You can. I didn't raise you to let anything stop you. Even fear and especially uncertainty. Now, you've run away from your problems long enough. Go home and get your husband."

Ryleigh wrapped her arms around Mama Lil. "I love you. Thank you for loving me."

Mama Lil brushed her hair. "Always, Ry-girl. I'll love your baby just as much."

Chuckling, Ryleigh said, "Let's not get ahead of ourselves."

"I'm not." Mama Lil grinned. "I know that I'll be a grandma very soon."

"Mama Lil."

"Oh hush." She waved a dismissive hand in Ryleigh's direction. "Let's get you a new stack of pancakes. You need to eat."

After Mama Lil set more piping hot blueberry pancakes with extra blueberries and an extra butter in front of Ryleigh, she didn't wait. She'd finished half of her breakfast when she heard the bells above the door ring.

"Ryleigh, why are you here and not in Wellspring?" Ava said, loudly. So loud that Mr. Everly nearly dropped his cup of coffee. Ava stomped over to her. "Alright, spill. What's going on with you and Martin?"

"Can you not talk so loud?" Ryleigh bit down on a piece of bacon. "And sit your ass down and stop making a scene."

Ava sat down and swiped a piece of bacon from Ryleigh's plate. "Sorry," she grumbled. "You know I had to make an entrance, to put the fear in you."

Ryleigh couldn't help but smile at her friend. "That might work if I was actually scared of you."

Tossing a pack of sugar at her, Ava said, "Hey, I'm pretty scary."

"I agree. Just not to me."

Ava studied her. "What's wrong? You haven't answered any of my calls or my texts. Then, I hear from Owen that you're here and Martin is in Wellspring? Thanksgiving is in three days. You should be with your husband."

"I'll be with him. Tomorrow." Ryleigh took a sip of water. "My flight leaves in the morning."

When Ryleigh had initially flown down to Rosewood Heights, she'd purchased a one-way ticket. But after she'd finished her talk with Mama Lil, she'd immediately booked a flight home.

"Why did you come?" Ava asked.

"It's a long story."

"Good thing you have the rest of the day to tell me."

Ryleigh shook her head. Ava was nothing if not persistent. She could definitely beat someone into submission with her bossy self. "I'm spending the day with Mama Lil."

"Before you come by my house for dinner," she said

with a wink. "Either that or I'll be forced to sit here with you and talk until you give in."

"Oh God, please don't do that."

"Your choice."

"Fine. I'll come over for dinner. And we'll talk."

Ava stood. "Good. Now, I can go back to work. Be there at six." With narrowed eyes, she pointed at Ryleigh. "Don't make me come looking for you. I have long money, I'll find you."

Laughing, Ryleigh shook her head. "Get out of here, you nut."

Batting her eyes, Ava waved. "Bye."

———

Two. Fuckin'. Days.

Martin stared at his full cup of coffee. His life had spiraled out of control and he couldn't figure out how to fix it. So instead of talking to Ryleigh, he'd hightailed it out of town to Wellspring. Which wasn't like him. He didn't run away. He stayed. He fought.

"Excuse me?" Brooklyn Marshall knocked on his forehead. "Earth to Martin?"

With a quick smile, he glanced at his best friend's wife. "Sorry, I have a lot on my mind."

"Um hm." Brooklyn scooped a spoonful of grits out of her bowl and fed it to his godson, little CJ. "Except it's not like you to be so quiet."

Martin had arrived in Wellspring hours after he'd left Ryleigh—two days ago. But he'd made no move to let Carter or Brooklyn know he was in town. He'd simply holed up in his hotel room and worked. But Wellspring was a small town. And the hotel was owned by Brooklyn's sister-in-law, so it hadn't taken long for his friends to knock on his hotel door and demand an explanation. He still hadn't given them one.

"Okay, so it's been long enough," Brooklyn said. "Right, baby boy?" she cooed to her son and rubbed her nose against the squirming baby's nose.

Martin couldn't help but picture Ryleigh doing the same thing to their baby and a surge of hurt shot through him again. CJ laughed and he smiled. Even though they lived on opposite sides of the state, he saw them often. And he'd watched his godson grow like a weed in just under a year. The New Year's Eve baby had basically skipped the crawling phase and started walking.

"We've had two dinners, two lunches, and one breakfast since you got to town," Brooklyn said, "and you've yet to tell me where my girl Ryleigh is. I'm going to need you to say something other than she's busy."

Every time they'd asked where his wife was, he'd told them she was working. In reality, Martin didn't know what Ryleigh was doing. But thanks to the Find My Friends app on his phone, he knew she was in Rosewood Heights. The last time he'd checked—five minutes ago—she was at *The Little Rose. What is she doing?*

His phone buzzed and he picked it up. The message from Ryleigh surprised him.

Ryleigh: *I'll be there tomorrow. We can talk.*

Since he'd been there, they'd only exchanged a few texts. None of them amounted to much of anything. Just a simple "are you okay?" here or there. No "I love you" or "I miss you". Now, she wanted to talk and he wasn't sure he wanted to hear what she had to say.

Martin stared at his phone, agonizing over his response. He knew what he wanted to say but wasn't sure it was the right thing to say. He must have typed three different replies in a few minutes. Would her coming there help or hurt the situation? Right now, they couldn't afford any more arguments like the one they'd had two days ago. Decision made, he finally hit the send button on his last draft.

"Baby, why don't you give us a minute?" Carter suggested to Brooklyn, pulling Martin from his thoughts.

Brooklyn pinned Martin with a stern stare. "Fine. I'll leave. But I'm calling Ryleigh myself." She disappeared around the corner, humming a tune to a bouncing CJ.

"He's getting big, man," Martin said.

"Every day." Carter set his napkin on the table.

"How are you?"

"Good. It feels good having a little baby around. He keeps me busy, but mostly he makes me happy."

Nodding, Martin thought about how devastated Carter had been when he'd lost his first wife and daughter in a fire years ago. To see his best friend content with his life was a good thing. Moving to Wellspring had been the best thing to ever happen to Carter.

"Life is a trip," Martin said.

"It is." Carter leaned forward. "I feel like we're talking around the issue and you know that's not my style. It's not your style either. You should probably just go ahead and tell me what's going on with you and Ryleigh?

Martin shook his head. "She's in Rosewood Heights and I'm here."

"Okay?"

"Things aren't good right now. I needed some time."

"Time to what?"

"To think." Martin gave Carter a very abbreviated version of the events that had led him there. "I'm not sure I can get over this."

Carter sat back, assessed him quietly for a moment. "I'm not discounting how you feel at all. There's a lot to unpack with the whole surrogacy thing and the pact and her stance on children. But here's the thing...you and Ryleigh are together now. There's no pregnancy, no baby. Just you and her. Could you really give that up for a hypothetical scenario?"

"It's not a hypothetical scenario, man." Martin stood. "I'll be the first to admit that I hadn't really thought about having kids until the subject came up. But, damn. Am I supposed to be okay with never becoming a father? Do I just forget and pretend like it doesn't bother me?"

"Are you bothered by her choice? Or the fact that you don't have one?"

Pausing, Martin thought about the questions. "Maybe both."

Martin fully believed in a woman's right to choose what she wanted to do with her body. But he also believed in a husband and wife making big decisions together. There was no way to know if he would have reacted differently if she'd told him back in June, or even if she'd told him before they married.

"I get it," Carter said.

"I'm glad you do. Things change every minute for me." One moment he was upset with her for keeping the secret. Then, he'd get pissed about her unwillingness to budge. Sometimes, he found himself missing a baby that didn't exist, that he wasn't even sure he was ready for. Mostly, he just missed her.

"Seriously," Carter said. "Brooklyn is a trip every day. She challenges me to step outside my box, she implores me to open myself to new possibilities. It makes me uncomfortable sometimes, but I'd rather be uncomfortable *with* her than comfortable *without* her."

Martin paused. His friend, his brother had just said a mouthful. "Damn," he murmured.

"So you have to ask yourself… Can you walk away from her because of this?"

"I don't want to walk away from her," Martin admitted.

"Then, don't." Carter picked up his plate and walked over to the sink. "Fix that shit."

Is it that easy?

As if he'd read his mind, Carter said, "It probably won't be easy. There will be bad days, tense arguments. I'm sure there will be more nights when you feel the need to get some space. But the alternative…" He shrugged. "I don't even want to see you if you take the alternative route. I might have to kick yo ass because, bruh, your attitude sucks."

Martin barked out a laugh. "Shut the hell up. You and your wife should have minded your business and left me alone at the hotel until I was ready to come out. Don't blame me because y'all are nosey as hell."

Carter pulled a bottle of water out of the refrigerator. "I'm not about to let you wallow. I seem to recall a not-so-veiled threat from you to get my shit together a few years ago. I figured I'd return the favor."

Before Carter met Brooklyn, he'd nearly drowned in his grief over his losses. And Martin had given him a wide berth, until he couldn't anymore. That's when he'd basically ordered him to handle the software job in Wellspring, which had ultimately led to him meeting Brooklyn. Looking back, Martin was glad he was able to light a fire under Carter because he'd never seen his friend so happy. But he wasn't sure the fix would be so easy for himself. Carter was right about one thing, though. He had two choices—to fix this shit or not.

Chapter 4

I don't know if you coming here is a good idea.

Ryleigh must have reread that damn text a hundred times since Martin had sent it hours ago. He didn't want her there. *Have I really ruined everything between us?*

"Hey, girl."

Jumping, Ryleigh held a hand to her chest. "You scared me, Ava."

"What are you doing? I've been calling you for a couple of minutes."

"I was reading something," Ryleigh murmured.

Spending the afternoon with Mama Lil had centered her, made her feel ready to tackle her problems with Martin. But then he'd sent that text and tilted her world on its axis. Again.

"Dinner is ready," Ava chirped.

Unable to help herself, Ryleigh peered at the text again and willed herself not to cry. She'd already shed so many tears today. "I'm not hungry."

"But I made these mashed potatoes with extra butter

for you. I even sautéed the pork chops in butter. Just for you. You gon' eat something."

Ryleigh pressed a hand against her stomach as wave a nausea rolled through her. Closing her eyes, she took several deep breaths. *What the hell am I going to do now?*

"Hun?" Ava approached her slowly and squeezed her arm gently. "Are you okay?"

"No." She shook her head. "I'm not okay." Ryleigh shot her friend a sidelong glance. "I'm trying to figure out how I burned my relationship to the ground."

Ava gasped. "Oh no." Leading her toward a hallway, she said, "Let's go into my office."

Once inside the recently renovated space, Ryleigh plopped down onto a sofa and buried her face in her hands. Ava joined her on the couch and smoothed a hand over her back in a circular motion.

"Ryleigh, what's going on?"

"I'm so tired," Ryleigh confessed breathily. "I'm tired of living this lie with everyone. I told myself that I could go to my grave without ever saying anything. But I ruined my marriage because of it."

"Your marriage?" Ava asked. "Ry, look at me."

A moment later, she braved a glance at her concerned bestie.

"What happened?"

"I texted Martin and told him I'd be in Wellspring tomorrow. He told me he didn't think I should come."

Ava's eyes widened. "Seriously? Do I need to go to Wellspring and beat Martin's ass?"

Shaking her head, she said, "No, I'm the one that hurt him. Not the other way around."

"What did you do?"

Ryleigh blew out a harsh breath. "I had a baby and didn't tell him."

Bolting to her feet, Ava shouted, "What?"

"Please don't yell. I need my friend right now."

Without another word, Ava locked the door and returned to the couch. Pulling out her phone, she dialed a number.

Mac picked up a moment later, "Hey, boo."

"We need an emergency video chat," Ava said.

Soon enough, everyone was on the line. For a few minutes, they caught up. Raven and Quinn gave quick rundowns of their pregnancies. Ryleigh looked pleadingly at Ava, letting her know without words that she couldn't have this conversation right now.

"Mac? Ryleigh?" Quinn asked. "Do you have—?"

"Okay, we're not talking about this," Ava cut in. "That's not the purpose of this call."

"So what is the purpose?" Mac asked.

Raven leaned closer to the screen. "Is one of you guys sick?"

Ava squeezed Ryleigh's hand. "Go ahead, Ry."

Quinn frowned "Oh no, is it Mama Lil?"

"Why don't you just let Ryleigh talk?" Ava said.

Ryleigh took a deep breath and let it all out, telling them everything. By the time she was finished with her story, four pairs of wide eyes stared back at her in shock. "Say something," Ryleigh said. "Anything."

Raven shrugged. "I don't even know what to say."

"Me neither," Quinn agreed.

"I just really wish you would have told us so that we could have be there for you," Raven added.

"What I want to know is… How do you hide a whole damn pregnancy in real life?" Ava asked. "I know it happens in the movies, but a freakin' pillow does not conceal an eight-pound baby."

"Right?" Quinn agreed. "I have to say, you've always

been too secretive for your own good, but delivering a baby without telling us takes the cake."

Ryleigh blinked, surprised by their reactions. She'd expected them to be angry at her for not telling them, but once again they'd proven why they were her besties.

"And what about you, Mac?" Ryleigh asked softly. "What do think?"

Mac smiled. "I think I have a bad ass bestie. You're a freakin' rock star. You had a kid, after a hard pregnancy, and still managed to drop it like it's hot in Jamaica that summer."

Ava cracked up, pointing at the screen. "That's right. She did do that."

"She broke that thang down so hard." Mac laughed. "That lame ass guy she was dancing with followed her for the rest of the trip."

"We had to call resort security on him," Raven added.

Quinn shook her head. "I told her she needed to walk away from him. He looked creepy."

Ryleigh smiled through fresh tears. "You heffas are going to make me cry. Of all the things you could have said to me, you bring up Ocho Rios."

Wrapping her arm around Ryleigh, Ava pulled her closer. "We love you, sis. We got you."

And Ryleigh believed that with her whole heart. "What am I going to do about Martin? I fucked up."

"Yeah, you did," Mac said. "But we all fuck up from time to time."

"Seriously, though." Quinn took a sip from her mug. "I know you had your reasons for keeping it from everyone, and I'm not judging you. It's a big thing. I'm also not judging Martin for being hurt."

"I can't really judge Martin for being hurt either, sis,"

Raven said. "This does affect him. Do you love Martin enough to meet him halfway?"

"Of course she loves him. We wouldn't be here right now if she didn't. And he loves her, too. We just need to figure out how she can fix this." Ava crossed her legs. She had a reputation in town as a fixer. She was the Rosewood Heights version of Olivia Pope minus the ugly cry and the constant need for wine. "I think the truth is always a good starting point."

"Can I ask you a question?" Mac said. "Have you tried sex? A good blow job works wonders."

They all burst out laughing. Ryleigh needed this. She needed her friends. The way they'd accepted her flaws and loved her anyway made her heart swell with gratitude.

Quinn gasped, pulling her from her thoughts. "You know what?" She tapped her chin. "I read an article about a married couple going through something similar. Let me check my—"

Raven threw up her hand. "Listen, Quinn. If you bring up another article, I swear…"

"Wait, hear me out," Quinn insisted, her brow knitting in concentration as she peered at her phone. "This is important."

"No. Just no." Raven shook her head.

"Your stupid articles got us into this in the first place," Mac grumbled.

"Nah, Quinn can't take all the blame this time," Ryleigh chimed in. "Ava and her happy ass had a lot to do with it." She bumped shoulders with her friend and said, "I still love you, though."

"You better love me," Ava said. "I risked heart disease to make those damn buttery pork chops and mashed potatoes for you today."

They spent the next hour chatting. Ryleigh had listened

to all of their advice, but knew she couldn't say the things they'd suggested. When she talked to *her* husband, she needed to speak from *her* heart. Still, knowing that they had her back gave her a little bit more strength to do what had to be done. And she loved them for it.

Once they ended the call, Ryleigh picked up her phone and finally typed a response to Martin: *I'm coming anyway*.

————

"Thanks for coming to get me." Ryleigh's flight had landed at seven o'clock the next morning. Blake agreed to pick her up from the airport and take her to her car. She wanted to get on the road to Wellspring as soon as possible, so she planned to unpack, repack, and head out in the next hour.

"You're welcome," Blake said. "It worked out well. Had to have a reason for leaving this guy I met last night."

Ryleigh slid her carry-on into the back seat and climbed into the truck. Yawning, she said, "The flight was so bumpy, I couldn't get any sleep."

"I hate turbulence." Blake put on her turn signal and pulled off. Moments later, they were speeding down the expressway, headed toward her house in Canton, Michigan.

Ryleigh's stomach growled. Waking up late had ensured she wouldn't be able to stop for a blueberry muffin, and the bagel she'd purchased in the airport had been hard as a rock.

Blake eyed her from the corner of her eye. "Are you hungry?"

"Starving."

"Want me to stop?"

Shaking her head, Ryleigh told her no. "I'll get something at the house before I leave."

Blake took a sip from her travel mug. "I still can't believe what you told me last night."

When Ryleigh had called to let Blake know when her flight would land, they ended up talking for quite some time. Before she knew it, Ryleigh had shared the surrogacy story with her friend. Not surprisingly, Blake had offered her nothing but support.

"Me neither," Ryleigh agreed.

"I'm glad you're going to Wellspring, though. You need to go get your man. I'm sure he's walking around in that damn town alone and pitiful, attracting a lot of female attention."

"Really, Blake?"

Shrugging, Blake said, "Just sayin'."

Ryleigh shook her head. "You're crazy as hell. How's your family? Getting ready for Thanksgiving?"

"Girl, I've been cutting vegetables for days. How much celery can a person buy? Mom keeps texting, asking me to go to the damn store. I got three texts before six o'clock this morning. I'm ready for Thanksgiving to be over."

Giggling, Ryleigh listened as her friend told her all about the Young family tradition of overcooking and overeating for every holiday. "So, are you doing double duty now that Paityn is gone?"

Blake's oldest sister had moved to Santa Monica to launch a new business. After Paityn announced the move, Blake confided in Ryleigh that she didn't know what she'd do if she couldn't eat her sister's food on a daily basis. It was just like her friend to downplay real emotions. But Ryleigh knew Blake missed her big sister terribly.

Blake switched lanes and increased her speed. "Not really. Trust me, mom doesn't want me to fill in the gap. I burned the toast the other day."

"I told you to start paying attention when people cook, Blake."

"Why? I'm too busy eating. That is the best part of dinner, right? The food? Speaking of food... does Brooklyn really know how to cook?"

Ryleigh and Martin had spent a lot of time with Carter and Brooklyn. But now that she thought about it, Ryleigh hadn't really seen Brooklyn cook anything herself. "You know what? I don't even know."

"What if she doesn't know how to cook?"

"I'm sure she has it covered," Ryleigh said.

"I should skip our dinner and come with you to Wellspring. Oooh wee, those Wells siblings are fine as hell."

"Fine and taken," Ryleigh said.

Brooklyn had two brothers, Parker Jr. and Bryson. Blake was right, they were very attractive and very happily married—with children.

"Yeah, I know," Blake grumbled.

Ryleigh studied her friend. "Are you okay? You seem a little preoccupied."

With a shrug, she said, "Yes. I'm fine. Just a little burned out with work. Are *you* okay?"

"Hopefully, I will be." Ryleigh couldn't wait to see Martin. She couldn't wait to look him in the eye and tell him how much he meant to her. They'd had their space; they'd had their time to think. Now, they needed to act. "I just hope Martin will listen."

"He will," Blake said. "If he doesn't, I'll handle your breakup for free."

"Oh, so you have jokes?"

Blake cracked up. "I'm just kidding."

They arrived at her house twenty minutes later. "Coming in?" Ryleigh asked.

"Nah, I have to go to Meijer to buy Idaho potatoes.

43

Mom had a fit when I brought home a ten pound bag of Yukon Gold potatoes."

"What does she need them for?"

"Potato salad. I say a potato is a potato is a potato, but she acted like I'd committed a crime."

"Well…" Ryleigh shrugged. "I agree with your mom. You need a starchier potato for potato salad."

Blake waved a dismissive hand her way. "I don't care about that shit. I told you I just want to eat."

"I give up." Ryleigh leaned over and hugged Blake. "Maybe you will find someone who can cook or loves to order out like you."

"Don't play me, Ry. I'm not looking for anyone. Who needs all that drama? Not me."

"Alright, girl. I better go."

"Call me when you get to Wellspring." Blake gasped. "Oh, I forgot to give you this. From Paityn."

Blake handed Ryleigh a little sample container filled with some sort of cream. She knew Paityn had developed a line of sexual enhancement products and suspected one of her creations was inside that container. "What's this?" she asked.

"*That Ish.*"

Ryleigh read the label. Holding it up, she asked, "Is this that stuff you were telling me about?"

"Yes, it's *that shit* I was telling you about. And believe me, this clit cream lives up to the hype. Make sure you try it out. Today."

"When am I supposed to try it out? While I'm driving?"

"Not unless you want to get in an accident. But since you told me you haven't had any in a while, you can try it out when you get there."

"I'm hoping I don't need it." Ryleigh wanted more than some damn cream. She wanted Martin.

"Yeah, but you can never have enough orgasms. You might need that shit for when Martin is traveling or something like that."

Ryleigh got out of the car. "Bye, girl. I'll text you when I get there." She started to walk away when Blake called out to her. Turning around, Ryleigh said, "Yes?"

"Just so you know, I truly believe everything is going to work out with you and Martin. Just be open and be honest. The rest will fall into place."

Nodding, Ryleigh watched her friend drive away and wondered if everything *would* be okay.

———

Martin waited in the hotel lobby for Ryleigh. He knew she'd hit the city limits twenty minutes ago, and figured it was best to meet her at a central location. Because a room with a bed wasn't going to help them. Especially after the dream he'd had early that morning. No matter what had happened between them, he could still taste her, still feel her against him, still smell her.

The simple text she'd sent yesterday had sparked a surge of hope through him. If she'd willingly ignored his suggestion to stay away, maybe things weren't as bleak as they seemed twenty-four hours ago. Martin already knew what he wanted. He'd agonized for days about how his life would work without her. The simple answer was it wouldn't. Carter was right. Leaving her, walking away from his marriage, was an alternative he couldn't even entertain. It still didn't mean they could just jump back in without another hard conversation.

Scrubbing a hand over his face, he checked her GPS

again. He felt like a stalker watching her little "dot" inch toward his "dot", but it had been his only connection to her over the last few days, his only acknowledgment that she was still safe—at least physically. Emotionally? The jury was still out. If she felt even a little bit like how he felt, she wasn't safe.

Brooklyn entered the hotel lobby, a huge smile on her face. She spotted him immediately and waved. But she made no move to approach him, which was odd. Instead, she turned toward the door and motioned to someone on the outside. Seconds later, Ryleigh strolled into the building.

Martin had to remember to breathe, because even at a distance, his wife was stunning. Beautiful from head to toe in black skinny jeans, an oversized sweater, and the boots he'd purchased for her birthday months ago. Flashes of his dream filtered through his mind. *Damn, I want her.*

The decision to talk on neutral ground had been the best one because the way his body had responded to the mere sight of her... Hopefully, things went well today because he wanted to make love to his wife. *It's been too long.* And he was far too horny —and hard—to be in close proximity to her without the buffer of the public. Even then, he might not be deterred.

Brooklyn pointed to him, and Ryleigh turned. The whisper of a smile crept across her face. The two ladies gave each other a quick hug and Ryleigh headed toward him. He stood finally and met her halfway. *Signal of what's to come?*

"Hey," she whispered.

Damn it. Even the sound of her of voice made him want her, ache for her.

"Hi." He swallowed. Up close, she was even more

beautiful. He fought the urge to touch her, to trace his fingers over her cheek, to pull her to him for a kiss.

Ryleigh searched his eyes. "I'm sorry I'm late."

Shoving his hands in his pocket, he said, "Late?"

Nodding, she said, "Yeah." She glanced at her watch. "I was supposed to be here three days ago. But I was too stubborn to make that happen."

A sense of calm flooded him and he exhaled slowly. Unable to help himself, he reached out and brushed his thumb over her chin. The simple contact made him want to do more. Leaning in, he said, "Maybe late is better than never."

Ryleigh giggled. "Maybe. But let's not make *late* a habit."

Martin barked out a laugh. His wife hated to be late to anything. "Okay."

"Can we take a walk?"

He raised a brow. "Are you sure? It's cold as hell out there." Martin had gone out for a run that morning. November in Michigan wasn't for the faint of heart. The temperature had dropped twenty degrees overnight. "We can grab coffee in the café, if you want."

"I've already had three cups, so…" She held out her hand. "Can we?"

Martin hesitated a moment, before he took her hand. They walked down Main Street toward the courtyard in the near the Town Hall. He gestured toward one of the benches in the courtyard, and she took a seat. Sitting next to her, he rubbed his hands together.

Ryleigh shifted to face him. "Martin, I'm sorry." She entwined her fingers with his, bringing his hand up to her face. Kissing each of his knuckles, she moaned. That moan shot straight to his dick. "You were right. I've been a selfish bitch. There is no acceptable excuse for my behavior, no good reason to lie to you this entire time. I kept something from you that mattered to us." She let out a shaky breath. A tear spilled onto her cheek. This time, he brushed it away. "And I'm so sorry for hurting you. I hope you can forgive me for that."

Closing his eyes, he sucked in a deep breath. "Ryleigh, I—"

"Please forgive me, baby. Please tell me that we can fix this."

Martin leaned his forehead against hers, pressed his lips against her brow and pulled her into his arms. "We can try," he murmured.

They stayed like that for a moment, wrapped in each other's arms. Eventually, though, she pulled back. "I probably look like a hot mess." She chuckled.

"Not even close," he whispered.

Ryleigh smiled. "Before we go any further, I owe you the real truth."

He raised a brow. "There's more?"

She nodded. "For years, I told myself that I didn't want to have a baby because I didn't want to go through that physical pain again. The truth is, the day I gave Hailey to her parents was one of the hardest days of my life."

"I can understand why it would be hard." He figured it would be hard to hand over a life that had been forming inside her for months. "You did carry her for nine months."

"Closer to ten," she corrected. "But that didn't really have anything with *why* it was hard."

"Tell me," he said.

"I meant what I said. I wanted them to have her. At the same time, I wondered why I didn't have a connection to her. Like you said, I carried her for a long ass time. That little girl took me through some serious

48

changes. I joined a support group for surrogates and I listened to those women talk about how difficult giving the baby up would be for them. The group moderator would say how normal it was to feel conflicted. But I never did. I didn't bond with the baby. I didn't even think about it. When I saw her beautiful face, I didn't yearn for her to be mine. I just handed her over." She squeezed his arm. "Don't get me wrong, I love Hailey. She's a beautiful, intelligent young girl. She's so awesome. But I never look at her like I carried her. I've only seen her as their baby."

"Why was it so hard, then?"

She shrugged. "That's why. I felt wrong for *not* having those feelings."

Martin didn't know how to respond to that because he didn't really understand how she felt. "Because you didn't bond with Hailey? Isn't that the point?"

"Probably, but the fact that I didn't made me feel a little less human, made me consider the fact that I might not be mother material."

He tilted his head, studied her. "Really?"

"My parents never showed me any love because they were too focused on their own problems. I never felt accepted by the two people who were supposed to be there for me." Her chin trembled. "I thought I'd be like them, too cold to show emotion, too busy to spend time, too selfish to love a kid. The fact that I couldn't even muster up a tear after nineteen hours of labor, scared the hell out of me. It felt like something was broken in me, and I didn't want to take a chance of passing that on to my own child. So I told myself that I would never have a baby, that I would never risk putting a child through what I endured."

The pieces clicked together for him in that moment. Her unwillingness to have a baby had nothing to do with him or their relationship. It had everything to do with the damage that her parents had done to her.

"Ryleigh." He tipped her chin up so he could peer into her eyes. "Your capacity to love unconditionally is one of the things I love about you. You could never be your mother."

"I know. It's one of the things I realized while I was running late." She let out a strained giggle. "I'm not her. *We're* not them. It just took me over a decade to realize that."

Martin chuckled. "Like I said, late is better than never."

She nodded. "Now that I realize that, though, I *do* want to see a baby with your eyes." She kissed both of his eyelids. "With your nose." She brushed her lips over the tip of his nose. "With your mouth." Ryleigh pressed her mouth to his and placed her hand against his chest. "With your heart."

"What about *your* eyes?" he asked.

"Whatever. As long as it's healthy and happy."

Sighing, he said, "We still have a lot to talk about." Martin had heard what she'd said, but the baby discussion was still bigger than a short conversation on a bench.

"You don't believe me?" she asked.

"That's not it," he told her. "If a baby really is in our future, it has to be something we decide together, at the right time. Not because of the pact and not because you think it's what I want. It has to be good for us, when *we're* ready. Okay?"

Ryleigh smiled. "Okay. That's good for me."

Martin's gaze dropped to her lips. "There's one thing I want to make clear, though."

With a frown, she asked, "What is it?"

"We can't do this again. We can't go through months

of miscommunication, letting hard feelings build to a breaking point. I don't want to live like that."

She caressed his face. "Me neither. Baby, you're the best thing that's ever happened to me. I'm going to do everything in my power to make you believe, and show you that I'm the best thing that ever happened to you."

"I already believe that." Martin kissed her then. Hard and long. He only stopped to breathe before he went in for more, nipping, teasing, licking. *God, I want her*. He needed her. Now.

When she pulled back, he wanted to tug her to him again. Shit, he wanted to pull her onto his lap. But something told him the good citizens of Wellspring wouldn't appreciate such a brazen display of affection.

"Martin?"

"Yes?"

"I think we should go back to your hotel room."

Standing, he pulled her to her feet. "Definitely. Let's go."

They raced to the hotel, hand-in-hand, not stopping until they got to his room. He unlocked the door and pulled her inside, fusing his mouth to hers as he steered her to the bed.

They tumbled down on the mattress, removing their clothes hastily.

"I can't…" she nipped his bottom lip. "I can't get these tight ass jeans off."

Martin grunted. "Shit." He broke the kiss and peeled her jeans and panties off, flinging them across the room. He ran his hands over her thighs and cupped her pussy in his palm. "I think we need to get this one out of the way first."

He buried his face in her core, tasting her like she was his last meal, savoring her. It didn't take her long to come against his tongue, writing against him and screaming his name until she collapsed against the bed.

Climbing over her, he placed another kiss to her mouth and pushed inside her. "Shit," he murmured. "You feel too damn good."

"So do you," she breathed. "I missed you."

"Missed you, too." He bit down on her chin. "I need you."

Ryleigh smiled. "I need you, too."

Martin didn't have time for slow and steady. Hard and fast was on the agenda for this round. He picked up the pace, moving in and out of her, taking everything she gave him, and giving it back. They came together, clinging to each other as they fell over.

He never wanted to go so long without connecting with her in this way. Being with her like this was as necessary as air. Loving her was everything.

"Hey." He kissed her. "Open your eyes."

Ryleigh's eyes popped open. "Hey." She smiled. "You're so damn hot."

He laughed. "That's all you got?"

"No." She brushed her mouth over his. "I got you. I love you so much, Martin."

"I love you, too."

Epilogue

*R*yleigh's gaze fell to the grits in her bowl. Lots of butter, lots of sugar. Her eyes shifted to the pancakes on her plate. Homemade syrup coated the dough. Fat, juicy blueberries gleamed at her. The butter melted into the middle of the stack. And she… *I'm going to be sick.*

Jumping up, Ryleigh bolted to the bathroom, barely making it before she hurled into the toilet. Tears spilled from her eyes when she finished. *I really wanted those pancakes.* Last week, a piece of buttery cheese toast had set off a similar chain reaction that ended with her in the hospital—with an IV drip and a positive pregnancy test.

Martin poked his head in the door. "Baby? Are you okay?"

She shot him a shaky smile. "I wanted those damn pancakes."

Chuckling, he said, "How about we go with saltines and a Vernors?"

Pouting, she let him pull her to her feet. "It's Christmas Eve. Mama Lil made all my favorites."

Mama Lil had arrived just in time to get the good news. True to form, the older woman immediately started ordering her around, banning her from the kitchen and taking over everything.

He kissed her brow. "It's okay, baby. You can eat a cracker and imagine it's a blueberry pancake."

Ryleigh shoved him playfully. "Get out of here."

Laughing, he leaned against the vanity and watched her brush her teeth. "You're so beautiful."

"With a mouthful of toothpaste?" she mumbled.

"Yep. Even with that Crest coating your lips."

Ryleigh giggled. From the moment he'd heard the news, Martin had morphed into Super Dad-to-Be, able to calm her nerves with one beautiful smile. He was already the best husband and now he would be the best father.

He stepped up behind her and rested his chin on her shoulder. Peering at her through the mirror, he smoothed a hand over her stomach. "I can't believe you're pregnant."

She laced her fingers though his. "Me neither." She kissed his jaw. "That didn't take long."

After Thanksgiving, Ryleigh and Martin discussed babies and timing. Ultimately, they'd decided to just let things happen organically. He'd even agreed to help with the cost of the girls trip if she lost the pact. Thinking back, she realized that was the night she probably got pregnant. They'd made love for hours, in every position, in every room. She couldn't get enough of him.

"Are you ready to make that call?" he asked with a raised brow.

"I guess. Don't you think it's too soon?"

"Probably, but you already slipped up and told Ava."

Ryleigh had answered Ava's phone call moments after she'd received the news and told her friend the news. Her friend had immediately started planning the baby shower.

Mama Lil nipped that shit in the bud, though. Eventually, her friend and her *mom* had agreed to share baby shower duties.

"Okay." She sighed. "Let's do it."

He took her hand and led her into the bedroom. She climbed onto the bed and waited for him to bring her laptop over. Moments later, her besties were on the screen in front of her.

Holiday talk took over for a few minutes. Decorations, food, ornaments, and sex under the Christmas tree. *That crazy Mac.* Martin brought her a plate of crackers and a tall glass of ginger-ale. She bit into a cracker and tried to imagine it was a pancake. That shit didn't work.

After they'd opened their gifts in front of each other, Ryleigh listened to Raven talk about her planned Christmas dinner.

"Ry?" Ava said. "What are you up to?"

Ryleigh shook her head at her friend's obvious attempt to get her to spill. Sighing, she said, "Nothing much. Trying to make this cracker a pancake."

Mac frowned. "What the hell are you talking about? Is that a new recipe you're trying?"

"No. It's my life since I can't eat anything with butter."

Raven tilted her head. "You can't eat butter? Is the world coming to an end?"

"Do you have hypertension?" Quinn asked. "Yesterday, I read an article about limiting butter intake. Is that why you can't eat butter?"

"No," Ryleigh said. "I can't eat butter because the baby doesn't seem to like it."

Ava clapped. "Finally!"

"Oh my God, you're pregnant?" Quinn shouted.

"I am. Just found out last week." Martin could have knocked Ryleigh over with a feather when the doctor had given them the news. But instead of panic or fear, she'd only felt happiness. "I'm not that far along, but I couldn't not tell my girls."

Raven did a fist pump. "Yes! Misery loves company. There's a few things these babies of mine don't like either."

"Aw." Mac covered her mouth. "My contrary friend is going to have a baby?"

Martin laughed at that.

"Is that Martin?" Mac asked. "Tell him to walk his ass over here so I can see him."

Ryleigh waved him over and he leaned down. "Hey, ladies. Merry Christmas Eve."

"A Merry Christmas Eve Baby!" Ava said. "I'm so happy for you both."

A chorus of congratulations filled the room.

"Thank you," Ryleigh and Martin said at the same time.

He kissed her nose. "I'll be back. Have fun, y'all."

Once he left, her besties bombarded Ryleigh with questions. And she'd tried to answer all of them. Really. But she was ready to talk about something other than her uterus.

"So listen," Ryleigh said. "I wanted to thank you all for your support and for loving me the way you do."

"Shit, why are you trying to make me cry?" Mac said, fanning her face. "I just put my makeup on."

"And?" Ryleigh said. "I have to say it. Because I wouldn't be here without y'all. Years ago, I met four of the fiercest, most beautiful women I've ever seen up close. You're all so bomb I can't even believe my luck in the friend lottery. I love you, heffas."

"Damn." Raven dabbed her eyes. "See what you done made me do."

"I know," Quinn said. "It's just not right to make us emotional like this."

Ava didn't bother to wipe her tears. "Ry, girl, I love you."

"I love you more. Now, enough of this. I need to eat these damn crackers and take a nap."

Happy tears were quickly replaced with laughter. The ladies talked for a few more minutes before ending the call. Ryleigh burrowed into her pillow and took a sip of her soda. *Coffee would have been better*. But she'd agreed to limit her caffeine intake. *Or a Mimosa*.

Martin returned several minutes later. "That went well." He climbed onto bed next to her and pulled her to him.

Wrapping her arms around his waist, she snuggled into him. "It did. Thanks for giving me that little push this morning."

"Anytime, baby."

"Do you think I won't be able to have butter my entire pregnancy?"

He barked out a laugh. "Baby, you're silly."

She perched herself up on her elbow and peered into his eyes. "I'm so serious. What am I going to do without *Butter*?"

"How about we take things as they go? In the meantime, eat the damn crackers."

"Fine. But I don't have to like it." Ryleigh kissed her husband. "I like you, though."

"Like?" He raised a challenging brow.

"And love. I love you, Marty-Mar."

Martin chuckled. "Silly. I love you, too."

The End

COMING SOON

ONCE UPON A FUNERAL

Make sure you follow our Facebook page for the latest information on our upcoming work:

@onceuponaromanceseries

ONCE UPON A BABY

First comes love. Then comes marriage.
Then comes the baby... Pact!

Complete Series Order:

"*H*ey! I recognize that dick."

Emerie Cole stared at the cell phone that had been passed around to every woman in the salon. The giddy laughter in the room suddenly stopped. Several pairs of eyes landed on her; a gamut of emotions displayed in each of them. *Shock. Amusement. Concern. Pity.* The pity stares were the worst, though.

Her stylist, Kerry, snatched the phone from her and looked at the screen. "Stop playin', girl."

"I'm not playing," Emerie replied in a dull, flat tone. Because that's exactly how she felt in that moment. Dull and flat. And murderous.

Every other Saturday, Emerie, sat in the Hair Sensations salon, cackling with the ladies who shared stories of their dating escapades. It had become a ritual for them to pass around pics sent to them by strangers over the internet. But Emerie had never participated. Because she wasn't single, because she lived with her boyfriend of six years, and because she was committed to her relationship. *To him.*

Apparently, he wasn't committed to her on the same level. Instead of looking for a job, he was sending out dick pics.

"Sis, I'm sure it's not what you think," Kerry whispered in her ear. "It could be anyone's dick. If you've seen one, you've seen them all."

Except that wasn't true. She'd seen many, but there was only one that had a distinguishing birthmark on the shaft, right below the tip. She knew that because she lived with that dick every day of the last several years. The profile name was also a dead giveaway. *MOB Man*. He didn't even have the decency to hide his activity behind an unknown nickname. No, he'd used his initials and nickname for the profile.

"Rie, listen to me," Kerry said. "You can't…"

Emerie was sure Kerry was still talking, but she couldn't hear her any more than she *wanted* to hear her. Her thoughts were running a mile a minute, combing through the past few months, looking for any obvious signs she'd missed or any whispered conversations she'd tuned out.

Maybe it wouldn't have been so bad had she not been supporting them since he'd been laid off from his manufacturing job last year? Maybe she wouldn't be considering catching a case if she hadn't worked like a dog, picking up overtime and working more events than usual? Nah, she would have been pissed either way. Because this was some straight bullshit.

Emerie shook her head; freeing it of those thoughts. No time for regrets or even a sad, sorry meltdown. Definitely no tears. Not even a slight tickle in her throat. But the more she'd tried to hype herself to handle her breakup business, the more she wanted to cry. The thought of all that time wasted working on a relationship that seemed doomed to fail almost from the beginning made her want to throw up. She'd changed parts of herself to "compromise" with him. And the kicker? She'd turned down a dream job for him, for their love. The same love he'd stomped into the ground a little bit more with every month... every day they were together. But this? The. Final. Straw.

"Rie?" Kerry stepped in front of her and jostled her with her knee.

Emerie blinked, focusing on her friend. They'd met in this very chair four years ago when she'd happened to walk into the salon for a cut and curl. Ironically, she'd just broken up with her last boyfriend and needed a change in her hairstyle then.

"Huh?" Emerie swallowed.

"Did you hear what I said?"

"I have to go." Emerie jumped out of the chair, yanked off the cape, and picked up her purse. "I'll CashApp you."

"Wait!" Kerry called after her. "Rie, your hair is still wet."

But Emerie didn't care. She just needed to get out of that damn place and away from the curious stares. Ignoring the calls, she dashed out of the salon and ran to her car.

It only took fifteen minutes to make the drive home. Along the way, she'd tried to think logically. What if there was someone else in the world that had the same birthmark? But even as she tried to make excuses, she couldn't make the pieces fit into a nice puzzle that would exonerate him. Deep down, she knew it was the truth.

When she pulled into the driveway, she took a centering breath before she hopped out of the car. The house was quiet when she entered, no signs of her boyfriend. Which was odd since he was *always* home. The man barely went out to the store or to the gym or to put in a job application.

Walking through the house, she checked the family room, the kitchen, then went into the basement—his man cave. He spent a disproportionate amount of time hidden away in this space. Emerie glanced back at the staircase, checking to see if he'd snuck up behind her.

Eyeing his computer, she approached it and sat down on the chair. By nature, she wasn't an irrational or insecure woman. In all the years she'd been dating, she'd never asked her man for his phone, she'd never followed him hoping to catch him in a lie, and she'd always maintained that if she ever had to do those things, the relationship wouldn't be worth keeping.

Still, she had to know for sure. She clicked on the mouse. The lock screen came up, and she tapped a finger on the desk, trying to figure out what he'd used for a password.

After two tries, she grunted a curse. Finally, she took a chance and typed in his daughter's nickname and birth date. *It worked.* The internet browser was open—to the very website the ladies were looking at in the salon. *Fuckin' asshole.* She scrolled through the many messages in his inbox. Apparently, he spent a lot of time doing shitty things on dating apps.

Her vision clouded as she stared at the screen. The number of women he'd been conversing with—exchanging numbers and meeting at coffee shops and hotels—was straight disrespectful. Now, she understood why they hadn't fucked in six freakin' months. He'd been giving it to random women he'd met in chat rooms. All the while, claiming to love only her. And she'd been a damn fool for far too long.

Standing on shaky legs, she took a few calming breaths,

said a prayer or two. Nothing helped. Livid didn't do what she felt justice. It just didn't seem to be enough of an adjective. Like, seriously... she wanted to hurt him. Which was why she made the decision to leave before he got home. Despite her earlier assertion, she wasn't trying to go to jail for hurting that nigga.

She grabbed the large suitcase she kept in the basement and dragged it upstairs, straight to their bedroom. She picked it up and set it on the bed. Opening one of her drawers, she grabbed the contents and tossed it in the suitcase. She emptied the others just as fast.

Stepping into the closet, she brought out several outfits on hangers and dropped them on the bed. She did all of this on the verge of tears. Thankfully, not one fell. Not even when she heard the side door open, and not when felt him behind her watching her.

"What's going on, babe?" he asked.

Emerie didn't turn to him, because the thin string she was dangling on was liable to snap.

"Babe." She heard his footsteps inching closer but didn't stop packing. He reached out, but she dodged him, brushing past him toward the dresser. "Rie."

She cringed at his use of her nickname. Only people who loved her could use that name. Now, she didn't count him among that group of people.

His hand on her arm stopped her. "Babe, what are you doing? Where are you going?"

"Away from here," she grumbled, yanking her arm from his grasp. She hurried to the bathroom and cleaned out her bathroom drawers. And for the first time, she got a full unabashed view of how she looked. She'd left the salon in such a hurry; her hair was a mess—one side straight and the other side wild and tangled. *Great.*

Emerie let out a shaky breath and one tear streaked

down her cheek. One. Fucking. Tear. Because she'd let that asshole ruin her "me day". Getting her hair done was one of the only things she did for herself on a consistent basis. She loved sitting in Kerry's chair, she enjoyed being pampered. And he'd sullied her salon experience with his community ass dick.

Steeling herself, she cleared out her shower cubby and re-entered the bedroom. He was still there, still looking like he cared.

She stopped, irritated that he was blocking her suitcase. Raking a gaze over him, she scowled in disgust. The black suit he wore fit his six-foot-one, two-hundred-pound frame perfectly. The wine-colored shirt underneath the jacket complemented his brown skin. It was her favorite color on him. Gone was the shaggy, unkempt atrocity that had been covering his face for the past three months, and it its place was a trimmed beard and goatee. Any other day, seeing him dressed like that—looking so fine, so clean, and so sexy —would have made her want to do naughty things to him. But not to-damn-day.

He stepped forward. "Rie, talk to me."

"What?" she hissed. "Get out of my way, Marcus."

"What's going on?" he asked. "Your hair—"

"Shut up, Marcus!" she shouted, slicing her free hand in the air. "Don't say shit to me. With your trifling ass."

Marcus frowned. "What the hell is going on?"

Emerie snorted. "Fuckin' asshole." The need to throw something at him reared its ugly head. She scanned the room, but of course, there was nothing around but little shit that wouldn't matter and the stuff in her hand. Still, she threw her bottle of shampoo toward him. It narrowly missed him. But she sent the conditioner, feminine wash, and loofah at him. And it was the loofah that landed, hitting him on the side of his face.

"Emerie," he yelled. "Stop!"

"You have made a fool of me," she growled, picking up a pillow and swinging it at him.

"What are you talking about, babe?"

Furious that he'd continued this deer-in-headlights act, she jabbed her finger in his face. "You're sending pics of your little dick to random women?"

The absolute truth of the matter was his dick wasn't that small, but once upon a time he'd confessed that *he* thought it didn't measure up. So, she knew it was a soft spot for him.

"I saw your profile on some raunchy dating app, Marcus. At the salon!"

"Look, Emerie."

"I don't want to hear it. Since you're obviously on the hunt for new pussy, I'll just get out of your way." She walked to the other side of the bed and pulled her suitcase to her. Closing it, she zipped it up and set it on the floor.

He stepped closer "Emerie."

She held up a hand, signaling he'd better not come any closer. "Don't," she warned.

"Listen, baby." Marcus scrubbed a hand over his face and the pained expression on his face nearly made her want to comfort him. But she stood still, rooted to her spot. "I don't know what those females told you at the salon. And I don't care. They don't know me. You do."

He's good. And if she hadn't seen the proof for herself, she might have believed him. "Obviously, I don't know you."

He reached out. She stepped back. Marcus didn't let that stop him, though. Cradling her face, he bent to kiss her cheek. She dodged the contact.

"Don't touch me," she said, smacking his hand away.

"Baby, please." He pulled her closer. "Believe me."

Shoving him away, she said, "That's the problem. I don't."

"No." He shook his head. "You can't do this to us. I'm not accepting this."

Frowning, she said, "I don't care what you accept. But what you won't do is get another chance to play me the way you've done." She swallowed. "I trusted you. I worked my butt off for us. While you stayed home and pretended to look for a job, while you took my kindness for weakness."

"Babe, I just had a job interview. I think I got it."

"Good, because you'll need to pay your own damn rent. I'm out."

She brushed past him and hurried toward the front door. She'd come back for the rest of her things later. Right now, she needed to leave.

Marcus followed her. "What, then? You're mad. What you gone do?"

"It's simple. I'm leaving."

"Where are you going?" he asked.

"Somewhere. Else."

Marcus hesitated. "This is some bullshit, Emerie. I told you about those bitches in that damn salon. Kerry is the worst one. She's always trying to down me to you."

"Just stop, Marcus. I saw the profile on your computer. I saw the messages, the promises of dates and sex. No need to keep lying. I already know you're guilty."

"Really, Emerie?" Marcus approached her and tried to take the suitcase from her. She pulled it back. "You're going through my things now?"

She grabbed her coat. He gripped the sleeve and they played a stupid game of tug-of-war until she let go. "You know what? Keep it. I can buy another coat. I can do better than I've ever done here."

"Oh, okay." He narrowed his eyes at her. "You're going to buy new equipment, too?"

She sighed. Emerie supplemented her income with her passion. Music. She worked as a DJ in her spare time. Her CD decks, her turntables, her mixers, her controller... there was no way she'd be able to take everything with her. Her heart hurt at the prospect of losing the investment she'd made into her second career. *I should have thought this through.* "I'll be back for the rest of my stuff later."

"Good luck with that," he sneered. "Since I have to pay the rent now, maybe I'll sell your precious equipment on eBay or something. I'm sure I'll get a nice price for that state-of-the art sound system you purchased last year.

She stepped forward. "Marcus, you better not."

He shrugged, stepping back with an evil smirk on his lips. "Don't tell me what I better not do. This is my house."

Emerie's body tensed and her stomach roiled. A mixture of dread and disgust warred with blinding rage for dominance within her. "Your house, huh. All I know is," she took a deep breath, "my shit better be here when I come back. If not, I will *own* this house. Believe that."

With flared nostrils, he advanced toward her. "Don't threaten me, Rie. Your father won't get anywhere near this house."

Emerie's father was partner at one of the top law firms in Ann Arbor. And he'd been waiting for her to leave Marcus' ass for years. Up until now, she'd kept her relationship between her and Marcus, but she wouldn't hesitate to go to her father if she had to.

"Keep telling yourself that," she grumbled. "Don't try me."

"Ah, I see now." He backed up. "You go through my shit; you walk out on—"

"What the fuck is your problem?" she yelled. "You did this! You cheated on me. Multiple times."

"Maybe you're the problem?"

Emerie rocked back on her heels. "Are you blaming me for your wayward dick?"

"You don't fuck, you don't suck… it's your fault I had to find someone else."

Fury clouded her vision. "Fuck you, Marcus. I had to work. Somebody had to pay the damn bills." Before she could think better of it, she picked up the potted plant near the door, not even caring that the dirt was wet and splashed on her. She flung it at him. He ducked, but it hit the wall and shattered into heavy pieces. Wiping her face, she fought back tears when she noticed the mud on her palm. All of her fight evaporated. Not only did her hair look crazy, but she'd more than likely smeared wet dirt all over her face. *I need to get out of here.* "Go to hell." Swinging the door open, she walked out.

Excerpt: Her Little Secret
WOMEN OF PARK MANOR

―――――――――

*I*f Paityn could ban two words, *fuck* and *shit* would be it. One made her think of toilets. The other? Well, let's just say she didn't need to be reminded of something she hadn't been blessed to do in years. And for the last ten minutes, she'd listened to her sister string those same two words together in varying combinations.

"Girl! Enough!" Paityn shouted, cutting her sister off mid-curse. "Road rage is really a thing. Get help." Pulling two sets of new sheets out of the dryer, she walked into one of the spare bedrooms and dropped the bedding on the mattress.

"Shit, I need to vent," Blake yelled. "It's your fuckin' fault I'm in this predicament. Michigan traffic doesn't make me want to kill someone."

Unable to help herself, Paityn giggled at her younger sister's antics. "You're a mess."

"Hey, I can only be me," Blake said.

The loud blare of the car horn followed by another colorful curse had her shaking her head in amusement. Some things would never change. Trump was still an asshole, she still couldn't eat beans to save her life, and Blake Young still had a potty mouth.

"I'm hanging up," Paityn told her sister. "I have stuff to do before you get here."

When "the brats" told her they were coming for a visit during the Memorial Day holiday, Paityn was ecstatic. Since her cross-country move, she'd seen her sisters countless times thanks to technology. But air kisses and virtual hugs didn't replace real face-to-face contact.

"Paityn?" Bliss called through the phone. She noted the rasp in her baby sister's voice, as if she'd been sleeping. "Are you making something for dinner? I'm hungry."

"Yes, ma'am." She walked the other set of sheets to the third bedroom and dumped them on the bed. "I'm making reservations. At this new Cuban restaurant Rissa told me about."

"Damn," Bliss muttered. "Will you at least cook breakfast in the morning?"

"You're so greedy," Blake said. "You just ate a whole foot-long sub and half of mine."

"I can't help it," Bliss shouted.

"I'm starting to think you're only here because you want me to cook for you." Paityn hurried to the kitchen and opened the oven. The homemade peach cobbler she'd prepared was almost done, Blake's favorite.

"No, I'm here because I miss you," Bliss said, just as Blake shouted another obscenity at a driver.

"That's good to hear." She also checked the macaroni and cheese baking in the bottom oven. *My favorite.*

"I wish Dallas could have come," Bliss mused. "I tried to get her to cancel her plans."

Paityn lifted the top off the pot on the stovetop, stirring the mustard and turnip greens a bit before she turned down the heat. "I do, too. But I'm not mad at her for taking a vacation out of the country. It's about time." She glanced at the Instant Pot on the countertop, noting the remaining time on the pulled pork, Bliss' favorite.

The truth? She did have reservations for dinner and dancing. Tomorrow. But, tonight, she also wanted to spoil her sisters a little. And it had been a while since she'd cooked anything of substance.

Growing up the second oldest child of a world-renowned couple, known for mending relationships and teaching others to parent, had a unique set of challenges. Partly because it was hard to live in her parents' shadows, but mostly because there were eight of them. Yes, Stewart and Victoria Young had eight damn children—willingly and happily. Paityn was the responsible sister, the oldest daughter, always offering a plate of food, a hand to hold, and a shoulder to cry on.

"Duke is pissed you didn't invite him," Bliss said.

Paityn laughed, thinking of the phone call she'd received from her brother earlier that morning. "I didn't invite y'all."

"But you're glad we're here," Blake added.

"I am, but I'm hanging up. I gave the concierge your names, so you should be able to come up without any problems. Don't kill anybody, Blake. See you soon."

Paityn ended the call after her sisters screamed good-bye. Shaking her head, she turned the dishwasher on and poured a glass of wine. When the oven timer went off, she pulled the dessert out and set it atop the island. The smell of peaches and cinnamon wafted to her nose and she resisted the urge to taste the cobbler.

She scanned the notes she'd jotted down earlier that day. The clitoral cream she'd hoped to perfect had been harder than she originally thought. Between her work as a sex therapist and her science background, it should have been a no brainer. Yet, she'd failed to even achieve the big "O" for the first two batches she'd made. Biting her thumbnail, she pondered her choice of ingredients. Maybe she'd used too much sodium benzoate?

Paityn scribbled an idea on the notepad and eyed the prototype she'd created. It was the fifth dildo she'd created and, by far, the best. She couldn't wait to show Blake and Bliss, which was why it was out in the open and not in her makeshift office-slash-lab.

Once Paityn had decided every woman needed a big ass dick, the wheels started spinning and a business idea formed. Paityn knew there were other sex aids on the market, entire stores dedicated to the business of pleasure, but she'd jumped in anyway. Now she was preparing to pitch her brand of sexual enhancement products.

When her stomach growled, Paityn glanced over at the peach cobbler. *One spoonful won't hurt.* She grabbed a wooden spoon and scooped a heaping helping out of the pan. Before she knew it one bite turned into two. Then, three. *Oh my God.* Four.

Fortunately, the knock on the door interrupted her greedy moment. She licked the spoon as she headed toward the door. She'd figured it would be at least thirty minutes before her sisters arrived. The airport was less than fifteen miles away, but it almost always took more than thirty minutes to get there in the infuriating 405 traffic.

She wiped a hand against her black leggings and opened the door. "You're her—"

Only it wasn't Blake or Bliss at the door. It wasn't even Rissa. No, the very *male* visitor standing there, his fist poised to knock again, was someone she didn't know. But damn, he was someone she probably *should* get to know.

Swallowing, she plastered a grin on her face and hoped

she looked presentable. "Hi." When he didn't answer immediately, she swallowed. *Maybe the hottie is a creeper?* But it wasn't like she was in some random apartment building. The concierge didn't just let anyone come up to the top floor.

The stranger's eyes dropped to her mouth and she absently wiped it with her sleeve, hoping she didn't have peach cobbler crust on her face.

"Can I help you?" she asked.

He blinked and then blessed her with the sexiest smile she'd ever seen up close. Pretty white teeth, adorably deep dimples, and beautiful creases framing full lips.

"I'm sorry. My name is Bishop." He held out a hand, presumably for her to shake it.

Her gaze dropped to it, noted his long fingers and clean fingernails, but she made no move to touch him. *Not yet.*

"I work at Pure Talent," he continued. "Jax Starks told me about you."

Paityn's eyes widened. "Oh, yeah. Bishop Lang."

Why is my voice so high? Probably because when her godfather told her he wanted her to meet one of the best legal minds on his team, she'd assumed it was an old, graying grandfather. A man that golfed on his off days and spent weekends at some highbrow country club drinking Burnt Martinis or scotch on the rocks. Not this fine ass man with smooth dark skin and a body that made her want to sing, "Do me, Baby". Because she was sure he'd be able to handle the job in a way no one ever had before. *Focus, Paityn.*

"Yes, that's me." His tongue darted out to wet his lips. "I live in the building and figured I'd come up and introduce myself."

Unable to turn away, she nodded. "Right. I think Uncle Jax did tell me that."

Briefly, she wondered if this was even a good idea, considering she couldn't stop staring at him. How would she be able to concentrate on business? But she trusted her godfather's judgment because he had never failed her and always had her best interests at heart.

From an early age, Paityn learned that blood didn't make family. And it was because of relationships like the one her father and Jax Starks had. The two men had grown up near each other in Detroit, Michigan and had even pledged the same fraternity. They were brothers in every sense of the word, even though they were born to different parents. Jax was her godfather, but he was also her "uncle".

She finally stepped aside. "Come in."

He followed her toward the kitchen. "Peach cobbler." The low groan that followed hit her right in the gut—or lower. "Smells good."

She gulped down the rest of her wine and dropped the wooden spoon into the sink. "I'm making dinner for my sisters." She turned the greens off and tried to recall every-thing her godfather had told her about Bishop. Clearly, she'd missed some things that he'd said. "I thought you were going to be out of town until next week?"

"I got back a little early."

Paityn leaned against the counter, meeting his intense gaze once again. "Cobbler?" she asked.

He looked down at the dessert and swallowed visibly. Nodding slowly, he said, "No."

Paityn frowned, surprised at his answer. Normally, a nod meant yes. "You sure? Because you look like you want some."

"I'm sure." He glanced at the pan again, before he looked up at her.

Tilting her head, she studied him. Something was preventing him from eating her cobbler. Did she want to know what? *Or who?* The need to know more welled up inside her. *It's the nature of my job to ask questions.* It wasn't his arms. Or the muscles stretching against the t-shirt he wore. The fact that he may be eating someone else's pie didn't bother her either. Well, not really.

Instead of probing further, she decided a change of subject was best. "Uncle Jax tells me you work in the business development department," she said. "But what else should I know?" Okay, so her attempt to sound professional came out more sultry than businesslike.

"What do mean?" he asked.

Clearing her throat, she added, "Because if we're going to work together, I'd like to learn a little more about your ass." Her eyes widened. "I mean, your experience?"

He chuckled. "I can give you the long version, or the short version."

Hello, sexual innuendo. She really did need to get some. Everything about this man and this interaction made her mind sink to the gutter. Paityn scratched her neck. "How about we start with where you're from?"

"Long Beach."

She opened the refrigerator and pulled out two bottles of water and offered him one. "Law school?"

"Berkeley." He took the water and twisted off the cap. "I've worked for the agency for fifteen years, and I've been instrumental in negotiating several business deals for agency clients. Jax has also entrusted me with many of his personal business matters."

"Good. What has he told you about me?"

His mouth curved into a smile. "He mentioned you were important to him and that I should take care of you."

She bit down on her lip. "I mean, about my business idea."

"Only that you were a sex therapist looking to start a new venture."

Paityn grinned, pleased that he didn't seem uncomfortable with her occupation like some men. "That's true. Did he tell you anything else?"

Bishop raised a brow. "No. I assume you will tell me the details."

"Right. I'll send you the draft of my proposal." She slid her notebook over and jotted down a note to herself. "I probably should have done this as soon as he gave me your email address, but I didn't want to interrupt your vacation. I know we always say we won't check emails on vacation, but we always do."

Ha barked out a laugh. "I don't disagree with that."

"Let me know when you're free to meet." She closed the notebook. "I have appointments during the day, but I'm usually free in the evenings." Paityn conducted her sessions online, via video chat or text therapy, which she'd found to be a great alternative to in-office therapy. Most of her clients loved the convenience and it allowed her to work from the comfort of her home, wherever that was.

"I'll check my calendar and get back to you. I have your numbers."

"Great. You'll have an email tonight. Not that I don't think you wouldn't read my proposal before we meet, but you definitely should. And preferably not in the office. In front of people."

The last thing she wanted was for a picture of her prototype to flash across his screen while he had someone in his office. That would be embarrassing, for him and for her.

Bishop frowned. "Why do I feel like I should be scared?"

Paityn laughed. "Because you should." She waggled her eyebrows.

"Now, I'm curious. Maybe you should give me a hint?"

"I would, but—" A knock on the door interrupted her explanation. "Excuse me. I have to get the door."

She ran to the door and opened it. Before she could say anything, Blake and Bliss surrounded her, hugging her tightly. Paityn wasn't overly emotional, but it felt good to hug her sisters, and she held on for longer than normal.

Finally pulling back, she smiled at the twins, noting the tears standing in Bliss' eyes. She brushed her cheek. "Don't cry."

"Please don't." Blake rolled her eyes. "It hasn't even been a month. Get it together."

"Leave me alone." Bliss elbowed Blake. "At least I don't have a black heart."

Paityn giggled. "Get in here." She pulled one of the rolling suitcases inside. "Are you hungry?"

Bliss patted her stomach. "You know it."

"I thought you weren't cooking," Blake said.

Paityn led them around the corner into the open living room area. "You know I wasn't going to let you come here without making your favorites."

"So, no Cuban food?" Blake asked. "Because I had my mouth set... Oooh wee. This place is gorgeous. Floor-to-ceiling windows, stunning artwork. And I love the color scheme. Everything just flows. Uncle Jax is doing big things."

Bishop glanced up from his phone and stood. "Hi."

Blake bit down on her thumbnail. "And apparently so are you," she muttered under her breath.

"Who is that, sissy?" Bliss whispered.

"And tell me he has a brother," Blake added.

Paityn rolled her eyes. "Shut up." She introduced them to Bishop. "He's an attorney at Pure Talent and he's helping me with my business."

"Oh, so you're helping her with the Big Ass D?" Blake asked, a wicked gleam in her eyes.

Bishop blinked. "Excuse me?"

Paityn glared at Blake. "He doesn't know about that yet," she said between clenched teeth. Leave it to her little sister to embarrass the hell out of her. "I'm sorry, Bishop. Don't mind her."

"Is that peach cobbler?" Blake asked.

"Yes," Bliss answered from the kitchen. She lifted the top off the pan. "And there's greens. And it smells like pulled pork. Yum."

Paityn shrugged when Bishop met her eyes. "Sisters."

"Right," he said. "I should probably get going, let you visit with your sisters. We'll talk."

"I'll walk you out."

He waved her off. "You don't have to."

"I do." Paityn walked him to the door. "Thanks for stopping by. I'm looking forward to working with you." She finally reached out to shake his hand.

When their palms met, she couldn't help but notice how the contact flooded her with warmth, from the tips of her fingers to her shoulders and throughout her body.

"It's good to meet you, Paityn." His husky, low voice made her want to lean into him.

She didn't, though. Slipping her hand from his, she nodded. "Right."

"I'll talk to you soon."

She nodded again. Because apparently she couldn't form any words.

Once he was safely outside the door, she exhaled. If every interaction with him ended with a handshake that somehow felt more like a kiss or a tender caress against her bare skin... *I'm definitely in trouble.*

Also by Elle Wright

Edge of Scandal Series

The Forbidden Man

His All Night

Her Kind of Man

All He Wants for Christmas

Once Upon a Bridesmaid Series

Beyond Forever

Jacksons of Ann Arbor

It's Always Been You

Wherever You Are

Because Of You

All For You

Wellspring Series

Touched By You

Enticed By You

Pleasured By You

DECADES: A Journey of African American Romance

Made To Hold You (The 80s)

Distinguished Gentlemen Series

The Closing Bid

Women of Park Manor

Her Little Secret

Carnivale Chronicles

Irresistible Temptation

About the Author

There was never a time when Elle Wright wasn't about to start a book, wasn't already deep in a book—or had just finished one. She grew up believing in the importance of reading, and became a lover of all things romance when her mother gave her her first romance novel. She lives in Michigan.

Join the Elle Wright Reader Group!

Connect with Elle!
www.ellewright.com
info@ellewright.com

facebook.com/ellewrightauthor

twitter.com/lwrightauthor

instagram.com/lwrightauthor

Made in the USA
Las Vegas, NV
01 February 2021

16903975R00069